ACCLAIM FOR *JEREMY BATES*

"Will remind readers what chattering teeth sound like."
—*Kirkus Reviews*

"Voracious readers of horror will delightfully consume the contents of Bates's World's Scariest Places books."
—*Publishers Weekly*

"Creatively creepy and sure to scare." —*The Japan Times*

"Jeremy Bates writes like a deviant angel I'm glad doesn't live on my shoulder."
—Christian Galacar, author of GILCHRIST

"Thriller fans and readers of Stephen King, Joe Lansdale, and other masters of the art will find much to love."
—*Midwest Book Review*

"An ice-cold thriller full of mystery, suspense, fear."
—David Moody, author of HATER and AUTUMN

"A page-turner in the true sense of the word."

BY JEREMY BATES

Suicide Forest ♦ The Catacombs ♦ Helltown
♦ Island of the Dolls ♦ Mountain of the Dead
♦ Hotel Chelsea ♦ Mosquito Man ♦ The Sleep
Experiment ♦ The Man from Taured ♦ Merfolk
♦ The Dancing Plague 1 & 2 ♦ White Lies ♦
The Taste of Fear ♦ Black Canyon ♦ Run ♦
Rewind ♦ Neighbors ♦ Six Bullets ♦ Box of Bones
♦ The Mailman ♦ Re-Roll ♦ New America:
Utopia Calling ♦ Dark Hearts ♦ Bad People

FREE BOOK

WHITE LIES

Jeremy Bates

Ghillinnein Books

WHITE LIES

CHAPTER 1

The storm began when she was driving north on US Highway 2, almost four thousand feet above sea level. The low-lying clouds, black and bloated, abruptly split open, as if slit by a surgeon's scalpel, letting loose a bellyful of rain. Flashes of white lightning and rumbles of thunder followed. Katrina Burton flicked on the windshield wipers. Soon the rain became a downpour, a sonorous drone so loud she had to turn up the radio so she could hear the song, something by CCR.

She stifled a yawn, then rubbed her eyes. They were getting sore from staring at the road for the past two hours, which continued to unfurl ahead of her like a long black carpet with no end. It was a tiny two-lane thing, winding up through the forested slopes of the Cascade Mountain Range in northern Washington. The pot of gold at the end was the town of Leavenworth, where she'd been offered a job teaching high school English.

Her buddy sitting on the passenger seat beside her burped—at least she thought it was a burp. He made some strange noises sometimes. She glanced at the boxer: six years old, fawn coat, white socks on his feet, black rings around his eyes, like a rock star who'd gone overboard with the eyeliner. He was snoring softly, the sound muffled because his snout was tucked beneath his forepaws. "Not nice weather, hey Bandit?" she said. He cracked open an eye and gave her a half-baked look. She scratched him between the cropped ears. "Rhetorical question, bud. Go back to sleep."

The Honda's high beams flashed on a reflective yellow road sign that indicated an upcoming sharp turn. Katrina eased her foot off the accelerator. The last thing she wanted was to slip off the slick road. She was in the middle of nowhere, and her phone's battery was dead. She'd known that before leaving Seattle, but she'd had enough things on her mind and hadn't bothered charging it. So if she did go slip 'n' sliding and found herself grill over trunk in a ditch, AAA would not be an option. She would have to stay put until another car came along, which might not be for a considerable amount of time. She'd only seen two vehicles pass her in the opposite direction during the past half hour, a small sedan and a tractor-trailer loaded with what she'd thought was raw lumber.

The turn hooked left. She tapped the brakes, slowing to less than ten miles an hour. Halfway around the bend, she was surprised to see the dark smudge of a person shuffling along the narrow shoulder. The person's back was to her, but judging by the height and build, it appeared to be a man. Her approach was masked by the storm because he seemed oblivious to the fact she was creeping up behind him until the headlights threw his elongated shadow ahead of him as if it had been spooked out of his body. He turned, arms folded across his chest to ward off the chill of the rain. He stuck a thumb in the air, using his other hand to shield his eyes from the rain and light. His red T-shirt and jeans were drenched. His dark hair was plastered to his skull.

Katrina drove past without slowing. She was a single white female, and it was a dark and stormy night. She'd seen the movies. But as her eyes lifted to the rearview mirror, and she caught the guy staring after her, something inside her shifted. What was he doing out here at this time of night amid a thunderstorm? Had his car broken down? Had he been in an accident?

"Dammit," she said, already easing the Honda to the shoulder of the road. Wet gravel crunched beneath the tires as she rolled to a stop. She glanced in the rearview mirror again and saw the guy hurrying toward the car. Bandit knew something was up. He leaped to his feet, his blunt muzzle jointing wide. Apparently he thought they were getting out to stretch their legs. He loved two things in life more than anything else: going for walks around the block, and roadside rest areas, especially those populated with unsuspecting children ripe for harassment.

"Not now, bud," she told him. "Get in the back." She patted the top of one of the suitcases stacked on the backseat. "Go on, go."

He made a disapproving snort but obediently clambered between the seats, settling down on the suitcase. Katrina punched off the radio—the DJ doing his spiel—and waited. Rain drummed on the roof of the car. The windshield wipers thumped back and forth, back and forth. Then the passenger door opened, letting in a burst of wet alpine air. The guy climbed in. The green glow from the cluster of dashboard instrument gauges illuminated his features: dark eyes, dark hair, handsome yet young, maybe early twenties. He was also taller than she'd guessed, six feet give or take an inch, though thin and bony. His knees touched the glove compartment.

He closed the door with a bang, then ran his hands through his dripping hair.

"Not a nice night for a stroll," she said, angling back onto the highway.

"Car broke down," he said. "Mind if I turn up the heat? I'm freezing."

"Sure." Katrina pointed to the temperature gauge, which he cranked to the maximum. A roar of warm, stale air blew through the vents. "What was wrong with your car?"

"Flat," he said.

"No spare?"

"No."

Katrina was about to ask him where he was going, but he tilted his head back against the headrest and closed his eyes. She supposed it didn't matter anyway. The farthest she could take him was Leavenworth, which was only another thirty minutes away.

Several miles passed in silence. The headlights cut two circular swaths of light out of the blackness, illuminating the ghostly trunks of the trees that crowded both sides of the road, creating the effect of traveling down a long, dark tunnel.

Katrina felt odd sitting beside the stranger, not speaking. Yet he was obviously exhausted, and she let him be. Gradually, her mind turned toward Leavenworth, and the bungalow she was renting there. She already had the keys. There were three of them attached to a Niagara Falls keychain: front door, side door, and a smaller bronze one, the purpose of which she wasn't yet sure. The real estate agent had given the set to her two weeks before when they'd met in a Starbucks to sign the two-year lease. The bungalow was only semi-furnished with a fridge, stove, washing machine, but not much else. There wasn't even a bed. The owners—an old couple who had moved to Sacramento to be closer to their children and grandchildren—had left behind a futon, which was what Katrina would use until the movers brought the rest of her belongings and furniture the next week.

Far off in the night sky lightning flashed, backlighting the bowels of the storm clouds. Katrina glanced at the hitchhiker and was startled to find his eyes now open, staring at her legs. She was wearing a skirt, which stopped short of her knees.

"What's your name?" he asked her.

She hesitated a beat. "Katrina," she said.

"I'm Zach."

"How long were you walking for?" She glanced at him again; his eyes had left her legs.

"A while."

"I mean, where did you get a flat?"

"Mile back, maybe more."

Katrina thought back, but she didn't recall seeing a car parked on the shoulder of the highway. In fact, she was positive she hadn't.

At this realization a golf ball-sized nugget of dread hardened in her gut.

"On Highway 2?" she asked.

"What's with all the questions?"

Katrina had half a mind to pull over and tell him to take a hike. She'd stopped for him in a storm. She'd given him a lift. And so far not a word of thanks—just a tone bordering on insolence. "How far are you going...Zach, was it?"

"Yeah, Zach." He coughed into the back of his hand, and she smelled Scotch on his breath.

Katrina's hands tightened on the steering wheel, and that little nugget in her gut grew a few sizes larger.

She looked at the hitchhiker expectantly.

"What?" he said.

"How far are you going?"

"Depends."

She frowned. "Sorry?"

"How far are *you* going?"

"The next turnoff," she said without missing a beat—and surprising herself with the ease the lie rolled off her tongue. She'd intended to tell him Leavenworth, but her altruistic spirit had vanished. She'd made a mistake picking him up, and thirty minutes in the car with someone who was not only rude but drunk suddenly seemed like an interminable amount of time.

"Lake Wenatchee?" he said.

She had no idea. She wasn't that familiar with the area.

"Yes," she said.

"You live there?"

"Yes," she said, as smoothly as the first lie.

"By yourself?"

"By myself?"

"Do you live there by yourself?"

She chewed her bottom lip.

"Hey," he said, holding up his hands. "Just a question. What's your problem?"

"My problem?"

Perhaps hearing the change in her voice, Bandit barked. The hitchhiker jumped, turning in his seat. The boxer barked a second time, louder than the first.

"You have a dog?" he said, facing forward again.

Under different circumstances, Katrina would have said, "He's harmless." Yet now she remained quiet, wondering where the hell this turnoff to Lake Wenatchee was.

"Lake Wenatchee," the guy said, tapping the fingers of his right hand on his knee. "Not much to do out there, is there, Kat?"

She was "Kat" to him now? And the way he said it was...she didn't know. Lecherous?

"You get lonely much?" he asked.

"No," she said curtly. She waited for his reply, for him to insinuate something else. And if he did, what would she do?

Pull over and demand he get out, that's what. It's my damn car after all.

"You know, Kat," the guy said. "You remind me of someone I know. Kandy. That's her name. Kandy with a K, like yours."

Just then a green road sign appeared in the high beams, announcing the turnoff to State Route 207 and Lake Wenatchee State Park.

Katrina felt woozy with relief. She pulled over to the shoulder and flipped on the emergency lights.

"Sorry I can't take you any farther," she said. "But the rain's died down a bit. Another car should be along soon."

Zach didn't get out. He just sat there.

"Give me a minute to dry off," he said.

"I need to get going."

"You like hockey?"

"Hockey?"

"I'm a Red Wings fan."

"I don't watch it—"

"What's your place like?"

"What?"

"Your place. On the lake."

She steeled her voice. "Please get out."

"Is it actually on the lake? Or back in the trees?"

Katrina's unease ballooned to full-fledged panic. What the hell was going on—?

Headlights appeared in the rearview mirror, two small pinpricks, which quickly grew larger, brighter, chasing the shadows to their burrows in the footwells and beneath the seats. For a crazy moment she considered jumping out and waving the car down. But then it was too late. The car zipped past, sinking them into darkness once more.

Zach turned in his seat so his body became square to hers, and for maybe the first time in her life she experienced the frenzied buzz of mortal danger. This is what you read about in the news, she thought: an unsuspecting woman picks up a hitchhiker who overpowers her, drags her into the woods, rapes and murders her.

Was that what happened to Kandy with a K?

Zach reached for her. She smacked his hand away. "Don't you dare touch me!"

Bandit sprang to his feet, growling.

"Hey, calm down."

"Get out!"

"Calm—"

"Get out!"

"Jesus, lady—"

Katrina unclasped her seatbelt, ready to hop out of the car herself. Bandit was barking madly.

"Jesus fucking Christ," the hitchhiker said. Scowling, he shoved open his door, got out, and slammed it shut.

Katrina stepped on the gas and tore away, her heartbeat matching the rapid whoosh-whoosh of the windshield wipers.

"My God," she whispered, trying to get her mind around what had just happened—or might have happened.

The heat continued to blast full power from the vents. She clicked it off with a shaking hand. Bandit stuck his black nose between the seats and whined softly.

"It's okay, bud," she told him, as much to calm herself as to calm him. "It's okay."

Nevertheless, it was only some twenty minutes or so later, when she saw the sign reading LEAVENWORTH, POP 2074, that she finally began to relax.

CHAPTER 2

"What can you tell me about this one?" Katrina asked, touching the leaves of a three-foot-tall strawberry plant.

"Oh, yes," the elderly woman said from beneath a wide-brimmed straw hat. They were walking side by side in the greenhouse out back of a nursery located in the heart of downtown Leavenworth. Dotted throughout the jungle of temperate and tropical plants were a good handful of fountains, sandstone statues, and garden gnomes for sale. The air was rich with the peaty smell of soil and the sweet fragrance of flowers. "We have several types of alpines. This is the white variety. Highly recommended since it doesn't attract the birds."

"How do the berries taste?"

"The flavor is very intense. They need to be eaten soon after they're picked, as they deteriorate rapidly when they sit around. They don't freeze well either, but they make wonderful preserves."

Katrina was more of a jam person herself, but she was always up for something different. After all, she'd left her old life and moved to a tiny town in the mountains. This thought unleashed a whisper of uneasiness inside her. "Okay," she said. "I'll take this one also then."

"Did you drive? Because I can wrap your plants to fit—"

"No, I walked. If it's all right, I'll collect everything tomorrow."

They returned inside and Katrina paid for her purchases. She scooped out several little fridge magnets from a bowl on the counter. One read, "Save our Earth, Plant a tree." Another, "Plant a little happiness." The third, "I ♥ my mom." She added the first two to the bill and returned the third to the bowl. She scribbled her signature on the Amex receipt and was about to leave the shop when she froze. Outside on the other side of the glass door, walking with his head down, was the hitchhiker. His hands were jammed into the pockets of his jeans, his hair blowing in the wind.

Katrina couldn't decide whether she wanted to chase him down and demand to know why he was stalking her, or slip out the back door. In the end she merely stood there, second-guessing herself. Stalking her? No, she was overreacting. Because even if he'd been crazy enough to spend the night tracking her down for whatever reason, how had he done it? She'd told him she lived on

Lake Wenatchee, not in Leavenworth. She'd never mentioned Leavenworth. She was sure of that. Moreover, she hadn't told him she was a teacher or anything like that.

So what was he doing here then?

There was only one answer, of course. He lived here. Not in Peshastin or Dryden or some other nearby town. Right here in Leavenworth. Hell, maybe they were neighbors.

"Dear?" the elderly woman said. "Is everything all right?"

Katrina nodded and left the shop. She glanced down the street, the way the hitchhiker—Zach—had gone. A mother was pushing a baby carriage, and a middle-aged man painting the sign outside his shop, but no hitchhiker. He must have turned down some side street.

Katrina started home. The September sky was a bright azure blue, scrubbed clean from the thunderstorm the night before. The wind was sharp and crisp, carrying with it the hint of autumn. In the distance, behind the gingerbread-style storefronts, the snowcapped peaks of the Northern Cascade Mountains towered majestically.

She turned off Front Street the first chance she got. Her earlier rationale aside, she couldn't shake the feeling Zach was indeed stalking her, ducking behind a hedge or garbage can each time she looked back over her shoulder.

The bungalow she was renting on Wheeler

Street was a quaint redbrick with white shutters and matching trim. It sat on a four-acre lot, set far back from the road and barely visible through the branches of two massive Douglas firs and a ponderosa pine. The grass in the yard was ankle-high. The flower garden was dead. The ivy crawling up the front wall reluctantly gave way to a large bay window. However, it would clean up nicely with a little work.

Katrina followed the stone pavers to the front porch, unlocked the door, and stepped inside the foyer, closing the door behind her. As an afterthought, she peeked through the beveled glass in the door. The street was empty in both directions as far as she could see.

She slid the deadbolt solidly into place.

* * *

Unpacking. That's how Katrina spent the remainder of the afternoon. Unpacking and making the house as comfortable as possible with the few belongings she'd managed to cram into the Honda. She placed her little African wood carvings around the living room and plugged her stereo system into a wall socket—leaving the stereo sitting on the floor, as there was no table to set it on. As she looked around the large room, she realized that even when the movers brought the rest of her belongings she would still need to purchase some additional items to fill the space. She looked forward to this. Unlike many other small towns, Leavenworth's main street was a string of pearls boasting fashionable clothing boutiques and chic galleries and European curiosity shops with names like Das Meisterstruck and Haus Lichtenstein.

After the Depression some eighty years ago, the Great Northern Railway Company had rerouted its railroad and the sawmill had subsequently closed, putting an end to the lumber industry and leaving Leavenworth little more than a ghost town. Thirty years onward, community leaders concocted a plan to remodel their ailing hamlet into the form of a Bavarian village, complete with traditional festivals such as the Autumn Leaf Festival and the Christmas Lighting Ceremony. Consequently, Leavenworth was now a medieval-themed village that attracted over a million tourists a year.

By five o'clock Katrina was getting hungry. She decided to open the last two boxes in front of her, then make something to eat for dinner, maybe the salmon she'd picked up earlier from the supermarket. She cut the masking tape that sealed the first box and extracted some paperback novels she hadn't read yet, a folder that contained recent credit card receipts, more books, and a thick pile of cards bound by an elastic band. These were the sympathy cards she'd received after Shawn's funeral. She'd donated all of Shawn's personal belongings of value to the Salvation Army, then disposed of anything else related to him except those items of sentimental worth, which she'd given to his parents. Nevertheless, she hadn't been able to let go of the cards. She needed to move on with her life, but she couldn't categorically erase all memory of the man to whom she'd been engaged to marry.

The second box contained her MacBook, a black nylon case that held her CD collection—Chopin, Mozart, Tchaikovsky, as well as some jazz and rock—a bunch of wires the purpose of which she wasn't sure, and her digital camera, which had gotten little use lately.

Tucked down at the bottom of the box were several framed photographs. She lifted them out. The top one was of her as a child: blue eyes bugging out of her heart-shaped face, blonde hair tied back in pigtails. She stared at the photo with the rusty, aged feeling you got when you reminisced, and a long-forgotten memory popped into her head, a show-and-tell session back in elementary school. A boy in her class named Greg—Greg something, something Greek—had shown a Japanese anime magazine his father had brought back from a business trip to Tokyo. Katrina's classmates had all thought the girls in the comic books resembled her, and for the rest of the year everybody had called her Japrina.

The remaining pictures were of her close friends and family. The largest one was in a silver frame and showed her parents, their arms around one another, happy, loving, the whole nine yards. Like Shawn, they had left her too early.

Two weeks before Christmas, while Katrina had been working on her teacher certification degree at the University of Washington, she had been summoned from the lecture hall to the dean's office, where the dean had explained to her that her parents had been driving along State Route 99 outside of Everett that morning when they'd struck a moose. The collision killed them instantly. The dean didn't go into graphic detail, but she later learned that her parents' sedan took out the moose's legs, hurtling the seven-and-a-half-foot tall adult bull through the windshield. The impact crushed her mother's rib cage and vital organs, as well as broke her neck and back. A tine from the antlers pierced her father's heart, pinning him to the seat—

Katrina switched off the memory, something she had become adept at doing over the years. Bandit padded over from where he'd been lying next to the fireplace and flopped down beside her. She scratched his head, grateful for his company.

The old-fashioned clanging of a rotary telephone made her jump.

For a moment she remained seated cross-legged on the floor. She hadn't installed a landline yet.

The ringing continued. It wasn't for her, it couldn't be for her, yet she got to her feet. As she narrowed in on the source of the ringing, she decided the call must be for the couple who owned the place. They'd forgotten to cancel their service and an uninformed friend was trying to reach them.

Five rings, six, seven.

Finally, Katrina found the phone sitting on a dusty shelf near the back door. The cord was stapled into the wall before it terminated in the jack located in the footing that ran along the floor. She picked up the receiver and said hello.

There was no response.

"Hello?" she repeated.

No reply.

The disconnect tone buzzed in her ear. Whoever it had been had hung up.

She replaced the receiver on the cradle.

For a moment she was spooked. She couldn't help but think of the hitchhiker. Yet she knew this was paranoia, nothing more. Even if he'd seen her today, which he hadn't, how would he have gotten the house's telephone number?

Katrina went to the kitchen to prepare the salmon but found she was no longer hungry. Instead she eyed a bottle of Pinot Noir on the countertop. It was a 2001 reserve from Panorama Vineyard in Tasmania, a gift from a friend after Shawn passed. She'd been saving it for...she didn't know...a special occasion, she supposed.

Nevertheless, given she didn't foresee any special occasions in her near future, and the fact her nerves were jacked, she opened it and filled a burgundy glass halfway to the rim. She returned to the living room, where she curled up with Bandit in the lone armchair and turned on the small TV that, along with the armchair and futon, had been one of the few furnishings left behind. She watched an episode of a syndicated sitcom, then flicked to Dateline, which was featuring a story about an allegedly dangerous fugitive on the run who was suspected to be in the Seattle area.

Katrina only saw the first fifteen minutes or so before her eyelids became heavy from the wine and she drifted into a dreamless sleep.

CHAPTER 3

Tuesday morning. The first official day of school.

Katrina arrived early to get settled in and to meet some of her coworkers. Walking from her car to the main office, she passed a few senior boys huddled in a circle, smoking cigarettes. They eyed her apprehensively, probably wondering who she was. Some of her past students—the younger ones at least—used to tell her she was too pretty to be a teacher, which always embarrassed her.

She got more looks inside from early bird kids already sitting at their desks or wandering the hallways. No one was at the office yet, so she made her way to the English department. She had a so-so idea of the school layout from when she'd visited for her interview in June. Skype would have saved her the two-hour-plus trip, but the principal was behind the times when it came to technology.

Only one teacher was in the staff room, a guy named Steve who showed her how to use the coffee machine, then gave her a lowdown on the troublesome students. At a quarter past seven the room began to fill up with other teachers, everyone introducing themselves to her. Then a secretary stopped by and asked her to come to the vice principal's office.

The VP's name was Diane Schnell. Katrina had met her during the June interview. She was a tall, no-nonsense woman in her sixties whose hair was pulled into a severe bun.

"Ah, hello, Katrina," Diane said, waving Katrina inside her small and cluttered office. She was standing behind her desk, looking out the window. A bookcase full of textbooks and three-ring binders dominated one wall. On the others hung several crudely done acrylic paintings by young students. "Have you found everything you need this morning?"

"The other teachers have been very helpful."

"Wonderful, wonderful," Diane said, though it was the type of "wonderful" that meant, "Enough chitchat."

Katrina remained standing just inside the door; she hadn't been offered a seat.

"I have a bit of news for you," Diane continued. "We have a new superintendent this year. He oversees a few schools in Chelan County. He's young, you know." She said this last bit in such a way that it was clear she didn't think young people should hold positions of importance on the school board. "Anyway, he's come up with a few ideas he thinks...well, I don't know what he thinks. What concerns you is that, as a new teacher, you will be observing some of your colleague's classes this week, to get a feel for how we do things around here. Today you and I will be sitting in on the first two periods. Since you're teaching freshmen, and they're in an assembly until ten o'clock, the scheduling will work out fine. Do you have any problems with this?"

an assembly until ten o'clock, the scheduling will work out fine. Do you have any problems with this?"

Katrina did. She had nearly eight years of teaching experience under her belt. Moreover, she would have preferred to use her free time to go over her lessons. Yet she held her tongue. Teaching was full of this kind of bureaucracy. It was easiest to simply go along with it then make a fuss. So she told Diane the arrangement was fine, then followed the VP to the classroom of a history teacher named Mrs. Horton. The woman accepted Diane's request to observe her lesson graciously, but Katrina could tell the unannounced arrival flustered her—and with good reason, for as it turned out, she didn't have much planned for the first day back after summer vacation aside from a general outline of the material the class was to cover over the first semester.

Regardless, Diane took about a half page of notes. While she was scribbling away, Mrs. Horton gave Katrina a look that said, "Get used to it."

Indeed, Katrina wondered what Diane's real motivations were for these impromptu visits: to give Katrina a feel for how other teachers ran their classrooms, or to give herself a Machiavellian excuse to appraise some of her staff.

The bell rang at eight twenty. Katrina and Diane were up and off, on their way to find their next victim. With barely a knock, Diane breezed into the second-period classroom that they would be observing, stated their purpose, and proceeded to make introductions.

Katrina was speechless. The teacher was staring at her with equal amazement.

It was the hitchhiker.

Katrina was sure Diane had noticed the uncomfortable introduction, but perhaps not wanting to ask any questions with twenty sets of eyes trained on them, she indicated for Katrina to follow her to the back of the classroom, where they took their seats.

Zach—or Mr. Marshall, as Diane had just introduced him—recovered from his shock at seeing her and began reading off the roll call. Lindsey? Here. Jacob? Here. John? Here.

More than once, when he was matching a student's face with his or her name, he caught Katrina's eye, hesitated briefly, then moved on. Katrina wondered if Diane was seeing these furtive glances, and she felt increasingly tense. What could she possibly tell the VP? The truth? That one of her teachers was a drunken creep who'd reached for her in such a way she'd believed he was going to—

To what? Rape her?

No, she'd seen the look in his eyes when she'd yelled at him. He was rude and sleazy, yeah, but not a rapist.

Nevertheless, he had harassed her, and that was something that was going to have to be discussed.

While Zach worked through his lesson, Katrina's mind drifted to an incident from her first year at Washington State, when she'd been living on campus in the student residences. Every dorm room had been equipped with computerized locks that required a keycard to open them. Each floor supervisor had a master keycard in case of an emergency in which access to the room became necessary, or in case a student lost his or her key. One night the supervisor who oversaw the second floor of the east wing, Charlie Reaver—known mostly as "Chubby" or "Reefers" because he was overweight and smoked a lot of pot—used his keycard to gain entry to the room of a pretty, bookish girl named Suzy Limmick. To do what? Who knew for sure? Maybe he thought a big fat guy surprising a girl sleeping in her bra and panties would be romantic. Suzy didn't think so. She freaked. It was a big scene, shouting, accusations, students sticking their heads out of their dorm rooms to see what all the fuss was about, everyone gossiping, speculating. Eventually the university performed an inquest into the matter. Chubby explained that he'd simply gotten the rooms mixed up, as he'd wanted to get into a friend's room to borrow a video game. He was cleared of any fault. Nobody Katrina knew believed the excuse, but because Charlie was a lot more popular than Suzy, she was the one who became ostracized for being a tattletale.

Similarly, Katrina began to suspect that if word of her and Zach's encounter on the highway spread throughout the school, and it became a he-said/she-said thing, he might end up the Chubby Reefers, she the Suzy Limmick—and that was definitely not the way she wanted to start the school year. Which meant the best thing to do would be to keep quiet about it for now until she could get Zach alone and agree with him to keep a lid on what happened.

Katrina returned her attention to the classroom proceedings. Zach was sitting on the corner of his desk, asking students what they knew about philosophy and getting a lot of blank faces in return. Admittedly, he was rather attractive with his dark, shaggy hair and dark eyes, and she was right when she'd guessed him to be in his early twenties, which meant he couldn't have been more than a year or two out of teachers college.

The fifty minutes slugged by. Zach's lesson wasn't great, but it was more organized than Mrs. Horton's had been. Even Diane seemed to be taking fewer notes. When the bell finally rang, the students clambered to their feet and made a general exodus toward the door.

Given the awkward introduction earlier, Katrina thought Diane might ask her if she and Zach knew each other, but she simply told Zach he had given an interesting lesson and then motioned for Katrina to follow her from the classroom.

Katrina did so happily, feeling Zach's eyes on her back as she left.

CHAPTER 4

Katrina was eating lunch at her desk in front of her computer browsing the internet when a teacher stuck her head in the door and introduced herself as Monica Roberts. She was young and energetic and wide-eyed as if she was seeing everything for the first time. Katrina liked her instantly.

"So you're the new teacher everyone is talking about, huh?" Monica said. "You know, you're more than welcome to join us in the faculty lounge."

"I would have," Katrina said, "had I known where it was."

"It's right by the library. I'll show you tomorrow. Actually, I have to run. Cafeteria duty. But I wanted to stop by to tell you about tonight. Did Hawk Eyes mention anything?"

"Hawk Eyes?"

"That's what we call Diane, the veep. Haven't you noticed? Black eyes and sharp nose and everything?"

"What was she supposed to tell me?"

"She wasn't supposed to tell you anything. I just thought she might've. Then again, she never comes anyway. We call it Back to School Night. It's nothing special. A bunch of us go to the pub for drinks. Wanna come?"

Katrina wasn't a pub person, but she figured it would be good to get to know some of her colleagues on a more personal level. "Sure," she said. "What's the place called?"

"Ducks & Drakes. It's on Front Street. Come whenever. Most of us head over as soon as we can get out of here. See you there!"

After Monica left, Katrina went back to browsing the web, but she couldn't concentrate on the news story she'd been reading, because an unsettling thought had struck her.

Was Zach Marshall going to be there tonight?

* * *

Ducks & Drakes was loud and standing-room-only busy. It was composed of one big room with what appeared to be a roped-off lounge near the back. Sports played on the TV sets while music boomed from speakers. Behind the bar, which had about a dozen beers on tap, was a blackboard with a "This Day in History" list, as well as the names of a couple of celebrities whose birthdays were today.

Katrina spotted the teachers on the back patio,

which offered a view of the mountains and the churning Wenatchee River, famous for its white-water rafting. They were crowded around a long table on which sat three pitchers of beer, two baskets of fries, and a tower of nachos dressed with the works. Someone had ordered a hamburger because on one white plate was a leftover crescent of a bun, a broken bit of patty, and untouched garnish.

A few quick introductions were made with the teachers Katrina had not yet met, then a geography teacher named Vincent topped an empty mug. He handed it to her, saying, "It's called Whistling Pig. I think you'll like it."

"Thank you," she said, accepting it.

He turned back to the person he was speaking with. Katrina sipped the beer as conversation droned around her. She was discretely searching the pub for Zach when she heard someone mention his name, laughing afterward as if Zach had been the butt of a joke. The guy who had spoken was a music teacher named Graham. He had a red afro, a handlebar mustache, and muttonchops.

"So he went to the bar and came back, right?" Graham was saying. "We were sitting down in the lounge, playing Double Dragon on the Nintendo they have hooked up in there, and I'm kicking ass, and Zach's doing all right, then all of a sudden the fucking dude spews all over the machine!" Graham laughed at this. "Seriously, like what the fuck? I think they banned him from here."

"Well, the ban is apparently over," said Monica, who was standing next to Graham. "I saw him over by the pool tables when I went to the bathroom."

"Playing by himself, I bet," Graham said. "What a frog."

Katrina excused herself and returned to the main room. The pool tables were up by the front, near an air hockey table, in a section of the room she had overlooked earlier.

She made her way toward them and found Zach not playing pool but throwing darts. He saw her approaching but ignored her, tossing one dart after the other at the corkboard.

She stopped beside him. "Hi, Zach," she said.

"Hey," he said, still not looking at her.

"I thought we could have a word in private."

He shrugged and threw a dart. "Go for it."

"Look," she said, glancing back at the table of teachers, "I don't know what happened back on the highway, but I don't care. Let's just forget it. New leaf, okay?"

"New leaf, huh?" he said. "I don't know about that."

She frowned. "You don't know about it?"

"A new leaf—it's not that easy." He threw another dart.

She lowered her voice. "Are you screwing with me, Zach?"

"Screwing with you?" The final dart. Triple fifteen.

"Do you remember what happened in the car?"

He finally looked at her. "I remember you kicking me out of it in the middle of a fucking thunderstorm, that's what I remember."

"You wouldn't get out when I asked you to, and you tried touching me."

"I didn't try fucking touching you."

"Hey, like I said, I don't care. It's over. Let's just forget about it."

"I want an apology," he said.

She stared at him, incredulous.

He refilled his pint from a pitcher of beer he was apparently drinking by himself. He tilted the mug to his lips, his eyes not leaving hers.

"*You* want an apology?" she said.

"For kicking me out of your car." He went to the board to collect his darts. Two teachers older than Katrina, though she couldn't remember their names, made their way to a nearby pool table and racked the balls.

"Fine," she told Zach when he returned, deciding if he wanted an apology, she'd give him his stupid apology. She simply wanted the night on the highway buried. "I apologize for kicking you out of my car. Okay?"

"Say it like you mean it."

"Give me a break, Zach," she said in a harsh whisper. "You're—" She glanced toward the teachers at the pool table. The one with the goatee and glasses was bent low over the felt, aiming with the cue, while the other one—beer belly and ruddy nose—watched on. She lowered her voice even more. "You're the one who should be apologizing."

"Where'd you go after you dropped me off?" Zach asked her. "You never turned off for Lake Wenatchee."

Katrina was about to tell him the truth, that she didn't live on Lake Wenatchee, that she lived here, in Leavenworth, but the look in his eyes made her reconsider. He was still bizarrely angry at her. Telling him she'd lied to get him out of the car might anger him further. He might make a scene. And she didn't want that, not here, not now, not with all the teachers around.

"I drove to the next turnoff," she said.

"And you doubled back?" He barked a laugh. "You think I'm an idiot?"

The duo playing pool was joined by a third person, a guy with a loud Hawaiian shirt. Katrina thought he'd said he was a chemistry teacher.

"Keep your voice down," she said.

But Zach continued as loudly as before: "You expect me to believe you live on Lake Wenatchee and drive, what, that far to school every day?"

Monica, Katrina noticed, had stepped inside the main room. She looked around, spotted Katrina, waved, and started over.

"Listen to me, Zach," she said, wondering how she'd gotten on the defensive. "If it really matters, I have two places, one on Lake Wenatchee, one here on Wheeler Street. Now would you drop this whole stupid thing?"

His eyes narrowed. "Why would you need two places?"

"This is finished," she said.

"You must be getting paid a helluva lot more than I am."

"It's finished."

Zach shrugged, then pushed his way past her just as Monica arrived.

"I guess I didn't have to come to rescue you after all," Monica said, watching Zach go. "I don't mind him too much. But you heard Graham. He drinks too much. Like, way, way too much."

Katrina shook her head. She didn't have anything to say.

"What were you guys talking about?" Monica asked.

"Nothing," she said. "Just saying hi."

"Come on," Monica said, taking her arm. "You're missing the fun."

They returned to the other teachers just as the waiter brought two more pitchers of beer. Katrina sipped hers, ate a couple of tasteless fries, and tried to enjoy herself. Twice she glanced down the table at Zach and saw him chatting with a female teacher.

About what? About her? About the encounter on the highway? Was he telling the truth or some altered version of events?

Monica, Katrina realized, was speaking to her, telling her about some of the art galleries around town, asking her if she wanted to visit one this weekend. She agreed, her reply robotic. Her mind was still parked down at the end of the table.

Finally, Katrina got up and went to the bathroom, mostly to walk off the nervous energy buzzing inside her like a bad caffeine high.

When she returned to the table, Zach stood and tapped his glass with a fork until he held everyone's attention. "A toast to our newest teacher," he said, raising his pint so beer sloshed over the lip. "To Kat."

People urged Katrina to speak, so she reluctantly stood. "Well, thanks, Zach," she said, clearing her throat. "As you all know, yes, this is my first day at Cascade High School. And from what I've seen of it so far, it looks like a wonderful place to work, filled with wonderful people. I look forward to getting to know you all better, and I hope we have a wonderful year."

This was met with nods and applause.

Katrina was about to retake her seat when Zach, still standing himself, said, "By the way, Kat told me she has a cabin on the lake. She also told me she'd like to have a welcoming party there this weekend, you know, like she said, to get to know everyone better."

The applause turned into cheers and a consensus that this was a fine idea.

Katrina glared at Zach. The toast had been a setup.

"A party on the lake?" said Bob, a math teacher. He was a bear of a man with a short, neatly trimmed beard and the booming voice of a tenor. "I think I can handle that!"

Suddenly everyone started talking at once, asking questions, making plans. Katrina was amazed at the speed it was all happening. Her mind raced. Come clean and confess right then? Tell everyone she'd only told Zach she had a cabin on the lake because he'd frightened the bejeezus out of her and she'd wanted him out of her car? Given everyone's inebriated state, they might laugh it off—or she might become a Suzy Limmick, the ostracized tattletale.

"Actually," she heard herself saying, "this weekend's no good."

"Why not?" Zach asked.

"Because." A second inched by, followed by another, as equally distended and painful. *Because you don't have a cabin. Just tell them that. You don't have a freaking cabin!* "Because I don't have any furniture," she said.

"So what?" Zach said. "Does anyone care if there's nowhere to sit?"

"Hell, no!" Bob said.

"How far is it, Kat?" Monica asked her.

"Half hour," Zach answered promptly.

"Not door to door. Must be twice that."

"I'm not driving," someone said.

"Me either."

"Not if I'm drinking."

"Cabs?"

"Expensive."

Just as Katrina's hopes were rising, Zach said, "We can get Lance to drive one of the school buses. If everyone chips in five bucks, that should cover it."

The excitement was renewed, with plans solidifying on the spot.

It was a circus. It was a nightmare.

Zach caught Katrina's eye and raised his beer in celebration.

CHAPTER 5

Zach cracked open his eyes. Darkness. Had he overslept? Was he late for work? No —the room was ink black, no morning sunlight slanting through the basement windows. He turned his head toward the clock. 10:03 p.m.

He rubbed the sleep from his eyes and sat up. The entire room tilted crazily. Christ. He noticed he was still fully dressed, jacket and shoes included. His first thought: he'd drunk too much again. His second thought: where the hell had he been? Then he remembered. Ducks & Drakes. He'd stayed until—when? He didn't know, but it had been getting dark when he'd wandered up his driveway, which meant he'd only been asleep for a couple of hours or so.

He stumbled to the bathroom and flicked on the light, which was way too bright. Then he took the longest goddamn leak of his life. He shook, tucked, zipped, and felt a heave in his stomach. He doubled over and vomited into the toilet bowl. He vomited again and again until his throat stung with gastric acid and his eyes watered with tears. He took a deep breath but didn't get off the floor. There was still more that wanted to come up.

Zach had a fear of public spaces, which made going to pubs and the like pretty damn tough. He had his first panic attack when he was thirteen at a festival at Peace Park in Seattle. The attacks began to occur more and more frequently, and he was eventually diagnosed with agoraphobia. It was a retarded disease if he'd ever heard of one, up there with werewolf syndrome, but that's what he had, what he had to live with every single day—

Up it came, the beer and the fries and whatever else was in his stomach, a burning projectile. Zach dry heaved until there was nothing left but fumes. But he felt better. He went to the kitchen and rinsed out his mouth with a glass of water. He gave the cupboards above the counter a perfunctory glance. There was nothing much to eat—at least nothing easy to prepare. He wasn't really hungry, but he wanted something to fill his stomach so he wouldn't be a walking zombie the next day. The Country Store Mini Mart would still be open. Same with the McDonald's across the street from it.

Zach carried his mountain bike up the basement stairs and started down Birch Street. The night was cool, the bluish-black sky filled with stars. Not for the first time he wished he had a girlfriend, a simple girl who liked homemade dinners and watching DVDs, so he wouldn't have to leave his place so much (and get shit-faced in the process to deal with his phobia).

Kandy came to mind, but she wasn't his girlfriend or even girlfriend quality; she was a stripper, and paying for her company wasn't the same thing as getting it for free. Kandy worked at the Rainbow Roadhouse, a bar-cum-strip club outside of town. The last time he was there he paid her for a dance, then—stupidly—asked her out. She told him some bullshit about not dating customers. He ended up spending the rest of his money—including his taxi money—on dances with other girls simply to spite her. All in all, it had been a shitty evening, and being caught in a downpour on the long walk home had made it even shittier.

And then Katrina Burton had picked him up.

Lying bitch.

The details of Ducks & Drakes might be a blur, but he remembered enough to know he didn't believe Katrina's story about having two places, one on the lake and one in town. It was just as bad as Kandy's lie about not dating customers. Did everyone think he was a fucking idiot?

He replayed the toast he'd made, telling everyone about Katrina's nonexistent cabin. Surprisingly, she didn't buckle like he'd thought she would. Which meant she was either stubborn, or she was actually telling the truth about having two places. Where was it she'd said she lived? Wheeler Street?

Well, maybe he would do some detective work and swing by. Because if she could afford a cabin on Lake Wenatchee, she would more than likely have something pretty grand here in Leavenworth.

He made a sharp turn back the way he'd been going—Wheeler was over on the west side of town, pretty much as far away as you could get from McDonald's, which was on the east side, near the school—and reached the street some five minutes later. Each property was fairly isolated from the next. Most windows were dark. In a few the bright flicker from a TV set seeped out from behind closed curtains.

Zach followed the road until it ended at someone's farm. He hadn't seen Katrina's Honda Civic in any of the driveways he passed, and he became more suspicious of her than ever. Had she lied about where she lived in town as well? He couldn't think of any reason why she would— unless she was a genuine pathological liar.

He started back down Wheeler. Halfway along he spotted her car. He'd missed it on the first go because it was at the end of a long driveway, partly hidden by the branches of a large pine.

The house was a modest-sized bungalow. He couldn't tell for certain, because it was draped in shadows, but it didn't appear to be in the best of conditions.

Not a hole in the ground, but definitely nothing special.

Zach was contemplating what this meant when

a light flicked on in the front room. A moment later Katrina passed before a large bay window, wearing something blue.

Before Zach knew what he was doing, he was off his bike and moving down the driveway to get a closer look. He stopped behind the Honda. He could see inside better. Some boxes were stacked against one wall, but aside from that, the room appeared to be mostly unfurnished.

Katrina appeared again.

She was walking back and forth, her head down, as if she was looking for something. The blue thing she was wearing was a terrycloth bathrobe, sashed at the waist. The throat was open, revealing the top of her cleavage. She bent over, stood, went to a hallway, flicked off the lights.

For a moment Zach didn't move as he wondered what he was doing—or was about to do. The words "trespassing" and "stalking" ran through his head, but he was pumped up on something, and he dismissed them just as quickly.

Then he was darting across the lawn, passing beneath the bay window. He turned down the side of the house. The shadows were deep and black, offering more cover. He crept forward, one hand trailing along the ivy-swathed wall. He felt frightened and electrified at the same time. His footfalls were silent on the soft grass. He came to the back of the bungalow and peered around the corner. Yellow light shone through a small window. He was about to start forward when the light went out, plunging the house into darkness.

That slapped Zach's senses back into his head. He blinked, feeling like a sleepwalker who'd just come awake to find himself standing in his neighbor's kitchen. His heart was pounding, and he was sweating.

He quickly backtracked the way he'd come, climbed on his bike, and rode home.

CHAPTER 6

Katrina woke at 6 a.m. and immediately recalled the events of the previous evening. Zach. Goddamn Zach the hitchhiker. She replayed how he'd announced to the other teachers that she had a cabin on the lake and wanted to have a party there this weekend, the chatter and plans that followed, and her reaction —standing dumbly by, unable to think of any excuses to stop the rolling snowball.

She showered, dressed, ate breakfast, then drove to Cascade High School. As she approached the English department, she had the unnerving sensation that all the teachers there were going to be talking about her party. This didn't happen. In fact, no one mentioned anything from Ducks & Drakes at all.

At noon in the faculty lounge—a Spartan place dominated by Formica tables and chairs— she was sure Monica or Bob was going to light a conversation that would ignite a discussion.

But the talk was mostly about the worst-behaved students and whether the cafeteria food was healthy or not. Today's lunch was a slice of lasagna, green beans, canned fruit, and vegetables and dip.

It seemed what happened outside of school, stayed outside of school, and Katrina was just fine with that.

After the last bell at two, she was in the parking lot, about to get in her car, thinking about stopping by the Italian place she'd seen the other day and getting a pizza for dinner, when Zach strolled by, pushing a bicycle.

"Hey, Zach," she said. "You okay this morning?"

"I don't get hangovers," he replied, appearing annoyed as if he'd been asked that question several times today already. A gust of wind tussled his mop of brown hair. He swept it away from his eyes, the way some of her students did, and she was reminded again of just how young he was. He continued past her.

"Whoa, hold on," she said.

He stopped. "What?"

She glanced about, then said, "You mind telling me what was up with that toast of yours yesterday?"

"It was just a toast." He shrugged. "By the way, I talked to some of the other guys today. Everything's still on for this weekend."

Katrina stiffened. "What do you mean, 'still on?'" she demanded.

"The party."

"Jesus, Zach! What's up with you? Seriously?"

"Hey," he said, holding up his hands, appearing contrite. "If you didn't want to have a party, you shouldn't have agreed to it."

"I didn't agree to anything."

"Yeah, you did."

"No, Zach, I didn't," she said. "Maybe you were too drunk to remember, but you're the one who suggested I have a party. You invited everyone."

"You agreed."

"No, I didn't, you little—" She bit off the insult. "You put me on the spot."

"Look, Kat," he said. "This really isn't a big deal. It's just a party. It'll be fun."

"Listen to me, Zach," she said, holding his eyes. "There is no party. Do you understand that?"

Shrugging again, he started away, pushing his bike. She got in the car, yanking the door closed too hard. She turned onto Chumstick Highway, making a hard right, cursing under her breath.

* * *

The wind blew Zach's hair away from his eyes as he rode his bike home from work. He had never actually brought up the party with anyone today. He'd only told Katrina that to piss her off—and he was glad he had. Because he'd seen the truth in her reaction. He was right. She didn't have a cabin.

She'd lied, and not only to him but to everyone who'd been at the pub.

* * *

Katrina pushed open the door to the small hardware shop. An electric chime announced her entrance. She took a few steps inside, then stopped. In places like this—men places—she always felt uncomfortable, out of her element, as though she was allowed to be there but wasn't supposed to be there. Even the smell of paint, metal, and wood seemed alien. It was the same feeling, she supposed, men had when they accompanied their girlfriends or wives into Victoria's Secret.

She glanced around, wondering where the nails would be located. Unlike in a supermarket, the aisles were not labeled. To the left of her was a pair of pumpkin-orange Black & Decker lawnmowers, their prices slashed, likely to move them before the snow started falling. In front of her was a pyramidal arrangement of paint cans. She stepped around the display and peered down the first aisle she came to. The eight-foot-tall shelves were lined with power tools and hand tools and other such equipment that looked like kitchen utensils on steroids. The next aisle was crammed with coils of wire and small plastic bins, each brimming with nuts, screws, nails, and several other gizmos.

She was crouched in front of the nails trying to figure out which size would be best for hanging paintings and prints when someone asked her if she needed a hand.

Katrina looked up and was surprised to find a tall, broad-shouldered man smiling down at her. She stood, smiling back. In place of a neatly trimmed haircut and clean-shaven face, he had raven-black hair pulled into a loose ponytail and about two days of dark stubble. He looked part Caucasian, but his slightly almond-shaped eyes and high cheekbones indicated a Native American heritage. He was wearing a short-sleeve button-down cotton shirt that revealed thick forearms covered with green-and-black sleeve tattoos.

"I'm looking for nails to hang some paintings," she told him.

"You're new to town?" he said.

"Yes, I am."

"Thought so," he said. "I haven't been here long myself, but I would have remembered seeing someone as pretty as yourself around, no question about it."

"Well—thank you, I think," she said.

"Drywall?" he said.

"Sorry?"

"The walls you're hanging your paintings on. Are they drywall?"

"Umm—I imagine so. Yes, I'm sure they are."

"Follow me." He led her a couple of aisles over and pulled a small package off one of the racks.

Through the clear plastic she could see a bunch of bronze-plated thingamajigs that looked like large fish hooks. He handed it to her. "Better than nails," he said. "You don't need to hit a stud. You don't even need any tools. Just whack one of them into the drywall and give it a twist. They transfer the weight from the hole to the wall and can hold just about any size picture."

She examined the package. "Monkey Hooks," she said, reading the label.

"The best." He handed her another pack. "On the house."

"Oh—no, no." She fumbled through her handbag for her wallet.

"Call it a welcoming gift."

She hesitated, then accepted the hooks.

He held out his hand. "Jack Reeves."

She shook. "I'm Katrina."

"Nice meeting you, Katrina."

"You too, Jack." She held up the Monkey Hooks. "Thank you."

"Anytime."

Outside the hardware store, the evening sun was setting, painting the sky amethyst purple and ruby red. A breeze carried the fresh, green scent of pine needles. The main thoroughfare was lined with Victorian Tudors with false half-timbering, scalloped trim on the pointed rooflines, and folk-art cutouts on the balconies. Shopfront windows displayed nutcrackers, dolls, beer steins, music boxes, and toys. Wooden boxes and barrels were everywhere, overflowing with colorful flowers. Take away the touristy vibe, and you could almost believe you were walking through a German village from centuries past.

Katrina, however, was paying the scenery little attention. She was preoccupied with the man she'd just met—Jack Reeves. He'd made her feel like a schoolgirl. It was bizarre. Not only because she'd known him for a couple of minutes, but because she had not felt an attraction to anyone since Shawn had died two years before.

She looked back over her shoulder. She could still see the cast-iron lantern that hung above the door to the hardware store, the light creating a yellow pool in the deepening twilight.

She picked up her pace. She had a ten-minute walk home, and night came quickly in the mountains.

❊ ❊ ❊

Katrina slipped a Queen's Greatest Hits CD into the stereo system sitting on the floor, then started hanging some of the paintings she'd brought with her from Seattle. The Monkey Hooks Jack Reeves had recommended worked great: poke, twist, voilà.

She was in the middle of leveling an oil painting she'd picked up at one of the galleries she used to visit when her cell phone rang. It was the first call she'd received since the mystery hang-up call the other day. She checked the phone's display. It was her younger sister, Crystal.

She pressed Talk. "Chris!"

"Hey, Kat. Oh God—Queen?"

"So what?"

"So lame, that's what."

Katrina turned off the stereo. "What's up? How's college?"

"It's only the third day."

"Your classes?"

"I think they're going to be all right. Except maybe this classical civilization course. It's at nine in the morning and the assistant teacher seems like a jerk."

"Can't you take it at a later time?"

"Doesn't fit my schedule. Anyway, just called to see how you'd feel about some company this weekend. You know, big old house, strange town. Must be a little creepy up there in the mountains by yourself?"

"You got one out of two," Katrina said. "It is a strange town. But it's a small house. I'm sleeping on a futon on the floor. Anyway, I'm fine. You don't need to worry about me."

"I'm not worrying. Just thought it would be good to hang out. Besides, I don't mind taking a weekend off to get away. Frosh is crazy so far. Fun —but like I said, a bit crazy."

"Well, if you don't mind sleeping on the floor, be my guest."

"Saturday okay?"

Katrina hesitated, remembering the party at the cabin she was supposed to be hosting this weekend.

But that was okay, she thought. Perfect, actually. She could tell everybody her sister was coming for a visit, and she would be spending the weekend showing her around.

"Kat?" Crystal said.

"Hey—sorry, was just thinking about something."

"If it's a bad time…"

"No, not at all. See you Saturday?"

"Cool! Looking forward to it." There was a ruckus in the background. Crystal said, "Gotta run. I'll call you Friday or Saturday morning to tell you when I'll be at the bus station."

They hung up. Katrina decided to leave the chore of hanging her paintings until tomorrow and went to the kitchen to pour herself a glass of the gifted Pinot Noir, which was still three-quarters full. She picked up the novel she was reading—a steamy thing about a blacksmith and a noblewoman—and went to the bathroom, where she ran the water in the claw-footed tub.

Unlike the rest of the bungalow, the bathroom had been recently renovated. The landlord had told her the owners had removed a wall to combine the bathroom with the laundry room. The washer and dryer were now in the basement, which was cluttered with a generation or two of forgotten belongings. Katrina had only been down there once, and she saw a *New York Times* newspaper on top of a stack of dusty boxes. It was from Sunday, July 20, 1969, with the headline proclaiming: "MEN WALK ON MOON."

Katrina added to the steaming bathwater two teaspoons of a vanilla-and-lime scented oil, lit a few candles, and undressed, tossing her clothes in the hamper in the corner. She slipped into the tub, sighing as the heat seeped into her muscles, all the way to her bones. She took a sip of the silky wine, closed her eyes, and found herself thinking about Crystal.

Katrina wished she could have been around for her sister more after their parents died, but it had been tough because Crystal had moved to Spokane to live with their grandparents, while Katrina had remained in Seattle, teaching. Katrina called her often and visited when she could, and she'd become concerned for her sister. Crystal had distanced herself from her friends, and she'd stopped caring about her appearance. Katrina had been hoping college would jolt her out of the funk she'd fallen into for so many years, but her suggestion to visit Katrina only a few days into Frosh Week was not an encouraging sign. She should be having fun, meeting people—not running away to hang out with her sister in a small mountain town.

Deciding to talk with her this weekend, Katrina set the matter aside and took another sip of the wine. She opened her eyes and caught a glimpse of herself in the mirror: hair tied into a messy bun atop her head, a warm flush to her cheeks. Not bad for twenty-nine. But she was in a world where young was better than old and she wasn't getting any younger. During the six years she and Shawn were together, she had never really given her age much thought. But now, single, she was becoming more and more aware of her invisible expiry date.

She set the wine aside, her eyes drifting up to the black rectangle hovering in the wall above and beyond her, where the window was situated. As far as bathrooms go, it was fairly large, fitted with a regular pane of glass rather than glass brick or some other such design that offered more privacy. She knew she would have to get a curtain for it at some point, but she didn't feel there was any rush, considering she had no immediate neighbors.

She picked up the novel, mindless of her wet fingers, and began to read.

* * *

The moon floated in the black-water sky, a big yellow eye that seemed to be watching Zach as he took the skullcap out of his pocket and tugged it down over his head so it covered his ears and eyebrows. He pressed himself tighter against Katrina's Honda Civic. His heart was knocking against his ribcage. His eyes never left the brightly lit front bay window.

He could hardly believe he was here again, doing what he was about to do. He knew he should turn around, go home, call it quits, but he couldn't.

Call him a sick fuck, but whatever. He wanted to see Katrina naked.

Nevertheless, as the minutes slugged by, and she failed to appear in the bay window, he became increasingly anxious. He was going to miss her again. The house would go dark—

Do it then. Go. Now.

Zach pushed away from the car and darted across the front lawn, beneath the heavy branches that blotted out the sky. He slowed when he reached the wall he'd skirted the night before. A light was on inside one of the windows. He stopped next to it.

For a moment he wasn't sure he could bring himself to look inside, because what if Katrina saw him?

No—that wasn't possible. Who sat at their window, staring out into the night? Besides, even if Katrina did randomly glance out, the glare from the light inside would only allow her to catch her reflection.

Zach looked inside.

It was the bedroom. Two nylon suitcases were stacked against a wall. A jug of filtered water sat on the hardwood floor, next to an empty glass. Clothes were piled in a messy heap in one corner. The only sign it wasn't home to a squatter was a neatly made futon mattress doused with an assortment of colorful pillows.

He continued along the side of the house until he reached the back corner. He peeked around it. There were two more lighted windows along the back wall.

He made his way to the closest one. It turned out to be the bathroom. Several candles burned, their small flames throwing jittery shadows on the beige tiles. Katrina was in the bathtub, submerged up to her neck in bubbles, reading a book, her head resting on the lip opposite the faucets.

Although Zach couldn't see anything good yet, he was already aroused, and he waited for her to readjust herself, part the bubbles, give him a view of something.

He must have been standing there for a couple of minutes watching her do little more than turn pages in her book when he realized something was wrong. It took him a moment to realize what. He wasn't looking at the actual bathtub; he was looking at the mirror, seeing the tub's reflection. Which meant the tub—and Katrina—were right on the other side of the wall, nothing but bricks separating them.

Katrina reached over the side of the bathtub and exchanged the book for a glass of red wine. The water frothed, revealing her breasts. They were round, full, the nipples a light shade of pink.

Zach pressed his face closer to the window, trying to see where the bubbles were thinning between her thighs.

Katrina finished what wine was left in her glass and held it in front of her by the stem as if she was contemplating something. Then she stood, a cascade of water rushing down her back.

Zach was so surprised he stumbled backward a step.

Something cracked beneath his foot. It sounded as loud as a gunshot in a funeral home.

Katrina's face appeared in the window. She screamed.

Zach was already running, skidding around the corner of the house, racing toward the street. He was halfway across the lawn when a dog barked. He didn't break stride but glanced in the direction from which the bark had come. On the sidewalk, near where the mouth of Katrina's driveway met the road, a man was walking a black-and-white dog, which was snapping at the leash.

"Hey!" the man shouted.

Zach snatched his bike from where he'd left it leaning against one of the big trees, hopped on it, and pedaled furiously.

Footsteps gave chase. More barking, closer.

Zach pedaled faster, half expecting the dog to attach itself to his leg at any moment.

Thankfully that didn't happen. The footsteps and barking diminished, then he couldn't hear anything at all except the blood thumping in his head.

He tore off the skullcap and stuffed it in his

pocket. The wind rushed past his face, turning the tiny beads of sweat on his brow icy cool. He sped down Birch Street and shortly thereafter reached his house, a ramshackle place with timber siding and a pointed roof. He went to the side door, carried his bike down the stairs, and dumped it in the corner, all the while his vivid imagination glibly explored how forensic guys in crime scene suits could prove what he'd done tonight.

He stripped off his shirt, pants, and shoes, and dumped them all in a green plastic garbage bag, which he shoved into the cupboard beneath the kitchen sink. First thing tomorrow he would dispose of it properly. Next he took a shower, not so much to wash away any dirt he might have acquired as to mark a return to normalcy. By the time he'd toweled off and dressed again, he felt calmer, more in control.

In the kitchen, he put on the kettle for a cup of coffee. While he waited for the water to boil, he told himself he was overreacting. A CSI team wasn't going to comb over Katrina's house. This was Leavenworth, not Miami. And it wasn't like he'd killed anyone. He'd just looked in a goddamn window.

Nevertheless, it wasn't as simple as that. He was a fucking Peeping Tom. That might not be as bad as being a rapist, or a pedophile, but it was still pretty damn bad. He'd lose his job, that was for sure. He was a teacher. Jesus Christ— would he make the local papers? He could imagine the headlines: "Local Teacher Caught Spying on Coworker!" or "Nightcrawler Busted!"

A whistling. The water was ready. Zach grabbed a mug with a picture of the Eiffel Tower on it from the cupboard, added a spoonful of instant coffee, then poured in the steaming water. He sat down with the mug at the table and went over everything that had happened, trying to remember Katrina's exact reaction. A curious expression, like she'd expected to see a raccoon, or maybe a deer. Her eyes widening when she saw a man in black instead. Then the scream. He didn't think she'd cried out a second time, but he couldn't be sure. His memories were already starting to form into one indistinguishable haze. More important, however, was whether or not there had been any hint of recognition in her eyes.

He didn't know. It had all happened too fast.

He shook his head.

What the fuck had he been thinking?

CHAPTER 7

Someone was knocking on the front door.

Katrina was still in the bathroom, wrapped in her bathrobe, wondering who it could be. Not the neighbors. They were so far away they wouldn't have heard a gunshot, let alone a scream. The Peeping Tom? But why would he be knocking on her door? Did he want to talk? Explain what he'd been doing? Apologize?

No, that was nuts. Anyway, it didn't matter who it was. She had to call the police.

She gripped the bathroom doorknob but hesitated. Bandit was barking—he'd been barking the entire time, she realized, though she'd only just tuned into it now—but she thought there was another dog barking as well. She listened. She was right. Two dogs. Burglar, rapist, murderer—or whatever category the Peeping Tom fell under—he surely wouldn't have brought a dog with him.

Curiosity replaced her fear. She opened the door and almost got bowled over backward by Bandit, who leaped up on his hind legs, his forepaws pressed against her thighs. She shook him off her, but instead of going for her phone, she went to the foyer.

"Who is it?" she called. Her voice wasn't as confident as she would have liked it to be.

There was a moment of silence before a voice spoke. It sounded concerned. "My name's John Winthorpe. I was walking my dog when I saw someone running out of your yard. I wanted to make sure everything was okay."

Katrina slid the safety chain in place, unfastened the deadbolt, then opened the door a wedge. A middle-aged and spectacled man stood on the doorstep. He was dressed in gray jogging pants and a gray sweatshirt. Katrina had only gotten a glimpse of the man on the other side of her bathroom window, but she nonetheless knew this was not the same person. The dog, a black-and-white Border Collie, snorted. Bandit went nuts.

"Just a second," she said. She closed the door, unclasped the chain, then swung the door a little wider. She grabbed Bandit by the collar and told him to behave. He whimpered but went quiet. "Did you get a description of the person?" she asked.

"Height and build, sure. And a brief glimpse of his face. Are you okay? You look shaken."

"I saw the guy too." She found it more difficult to articulate what had happened than she would have thought. "He was watching me through the bathroom window."

"Good God! Have you called the police?"

"I was about to. I...I just need a minute."

"Of course." John Winthorpe patted his dog. "Listen, if you want, Molson and I will wait out front, keep watch until the police arrive."

"Thank you. But I think I'll be fine."

"They might want to question me as well."

That was true, she thought. After all, he'd apparently gotten a better description of the guy than she had. "Well, if you don't mind waiting around..."

"Of course not. We'll be right out here. Just holler if you need us."

Katrina opened the door wider and stepped back. "Why don't you come in? Molson's welcome too."

As if to show his gratitude, the Border Collie stepped forward and sniffed her feet as she led them inside. Bandit began whining again, pleading to be let go. She released his collar so he could get acquainted with his new friend. The two dogs immediately began playing Ring Around the Rosie.

"Have a seat," Katrina said. "I only have one."

"I'm fine, thank you though."

Katrina retrieved her phone from the bedroom and dialed 911. She told the dispatcher what happened. The woman asked her several questions. What was her location? What was her callback number? Was there a crime involved? Had she seen the suspect? Finally, she was informed that an officer would be by shortly to take a statement. Katrina hung up.

"Someone coming?" John asked.

"Yes, right now."

Less than five minutes later a police cruiser pulled into her driveway. Katrina had the front door open before the cop—a burly man with black eyes and a thin mouth—had climbed the front steps. He introduced himself as Officer Murray. She invited him inside and explained what had happened. At his request she showed him the bathroom. The candles were still burning. She flicked on the overhead light and blew out the flames.

"So you say you were in the bathtub when you heard some noise"—Murray consulted his battered notebook in which he had been scribbling—"and when you turned around you saw someone watching you?"

"Yes," she said.

He crouched beside the bathtub and craned his neck to see up toward the window. "From this angle, wouldn't it have been tough to see out?"

"I was standing."

"But you were having a bath?"

"I was getting out."

"That's when you heard the noise?"

"I think he might have stepped on a plastic flower pot. I saw a few out back the other day."

Murray addressed John Winthorpe, who'd followed them into the bathroom. "You say he was tall and lanky? Anything else?"

"He was wearing a black pullover and black slacks."

"Face?"

John shook his head. "I didn't get a good look."

"What about footprints?" Katrina said. "He must have left footprints?"

"This isn't a murder scene, Ms. Burton," Murray said.

"Has this happened anywhere else?"

"Not that I can recall, no. Not recently at any rate." He stuck his notebook into his duty belt, took the peaked cap that had been tucked under his arm, and replaced it on his head.

"So that's it?" Katrina asked, surprised.

"I'll cruise around the neighborhood, see if I spot anyone who matches the description you and Mr. Winthorpe provided."

"And if you don't find him?"

"Unfortunately, there's not much I can do, Ms. Burton. Without a positive identification…"

"But what if he comes back?"

"He won't. Guys like this, they're in it for a quick thrill, opportunists. Now that he's been caught, he won't be back."

"You don't know that."

"No, I don't, but that's my professional opinion." Murray returned to the living room and tipped a nod at the bay window. "What I do suggest you do is get yourself some blinds."

"I intend to," she said. "Tomorrow."

"A goodnight to you, Ms. Burton. Mr. Winthorpe."

And with that, Officer Murray left. Katrina and John remained where they were, listening to his booted footsteps descend the front steps, the bang of the cruiser door, the cough of the engine as it started up.

"To protect and serve," Katrina mumbled.

John said, "I take Molson for a walk every evening around this time. If it means anything, I'll keep an eye out. Just lock up tonight, to be safe."

Katrina nodded, tired, deflated. These last few days suddenly seemed too much. She thanked John for his concern and showed him and Molson out. Then she systematically checked to make sure all the bungalow's windows were locked. She also stripped the sheets off the bed and pinned them over the bedroom window, using the Monkey Hooks she'd gotten earlier.

She wondered what Jack Reeves would say if he knew this was how she was using the hooks he'd recommended.

She changed into her pajamas, turned off the lights, then lay down on the futon. The night settled over her like a second blanket, but it was a long time before she finally fell into a fitful sleep.

CHAPTER 8

"Zach?" Katrina said, poking her head into his classroom. "I want to talk to you."

Zach was seated behind his desk, a Styrofoam cup of instant noodles in front of him, a pair of chopsticks poking out of it like antennae. He was dressed unexpectedly respectable in a jacket and tie, but he still looked too young to be a high school teacher.

"Yeah?" he said, frowning.

"It's about the party," she said. "I talked to my sister last night. She's coming to visit me this weekend. I'm going to be showing her around town, so there's no time for the party. And since you seem to know who wanted to come, I was hoping you could pass this information along."

"Well, I—"

"Thanks," she said curtly and left.

* * *

After the last bell, Katrina went to her car and pulled out of the school parking lot, waving to some of the other teachers she passed.

While heading into the center of town, she discovered that her palms were damp on the steering wheel, her stomach tingling with nervousness. She was heading to the hardware store to pick up some blinds—and all she could think about was Jack Reeves, and whether he would be working again. She tried to tell herself seeing Jack wasn't a big deal. If he was there, he was there; if he wasn't, he wasn't. Who cared?

Only she did. She cared. She'd been thinking about him all day.

As she approached the hardware store, she was tempted to drive past and look for somewhere else in town that might sell blinds. But she told herself she was being foolish and pulled to the curb. She checked her lipstick in the rearview mirror, then started down the sidewalk. She was still a good thirty yards away from the hardware store when Jack rounded the corner at the far end of the block. He didn't seem to see her, however, as his attention was fixed on the park across the street.

The gap between them disappeared fast. Then, to her surprise, he strolled straight past the hardware store.

"Jack?" she said when they were a few feet apart.

He noticed her for the first time. For a moment

she was sure he didn't recognize her, but then he grinned and said, "Well, hello! The hooks, right?"

"That's me," she said.

"They work?"

Katrina thought of them holding up the bed sheets over her windows. "Perfectly." She glanced past him to the hardware store. "You're not working today?"

"Ah, right. I, no—I don't actually work there. Leroy, he owns the place. He stepped out for a few minutes, asked me to keep an eye on things."

"But you gave me—"

"Don't worry about that. I paid for them when he came back." He waved the matter aside. "Anyway, I was just about to get a coffee. Would you like to join me?"

"I, um…"

"Hey, no problem. You don't know me."

"No, it's not that. I was just about to get some blinds."

"Tell you what. Join me for coffee, then I'll help you pick out some blinds. I'll talk Leroy into a good deal."

"Well—sure."

"This way," he said, touching the small of her back. His hand only remained there for a second at most, to turn her in the correct direction, but it sent a small zap through her body.

Jack chose a place called Café Mozart, which featured an upscale restaurant on the second floor. They were seated in elegant armchairs in front of a fireplace in which a small fire was burning. They ordered two lattes and made idle chitchat for a while. Given that they barely knew one another, Katrina thought the conversation would be stilted, punctuated with uncomfortable pauses. Yet Jack was relaxed and easy to talk to, and she almost felt as though she were speaking with an old friend. Then he dropped the bombshell.

He didn't live in Leavenworth; he was only passing through.

"When do you think you're leaving?" she asked him.

"No plans," he said with a shrug. "Hey—what are you doing for dinner? Have you tried real Bavarian food yet?"

"No, I haven't," she admitted.

"There's this place down the street. You'll love it."

She glanced at her wristwatch and was surprised to find it was already past five. She and Jack had been having coffee for more than two hours.

"I'm being too forward," he said. "I'll take a raincheck. Let's go look at those blinds."

"No...I...dinner sounds fun."

✳ ✳ ✳

After the old-world charm of Café Mozart, Katrina had expected an intimate candlelit restaurant with tables set for two. King Ludwig's, on the other hand, was a rowdy, family-orientated place. Murals and hand-woven tapestries covered the walls, while people danced on a dance floor and kids ran amuck.

Katrina let Jack order for them. Hickory-smoked pork chops and red potatoes for her, duck with plum sauce for him. The beer was strong, and it wasn't long before she began to feel tipsy—which was probably why she let him drag her to the dance floor and weave her around to the tune of German accordion music.

When they were back in their seats, Jack said, "*Gemutlichkeit*." He lifted his glass. "Good times."

"You know German?" She clinked their glasses.

"It was written on the menu."

Jack waved over the waitress—a young girl wearing a traditional dirndl dress, her blonde hair hanging down over her shoulders in long Goldilocks braids—and ordered them apple strudel for dessert.

"I'm enjoying myself," he told Katrina after the girl had left. "You're fine company."

"I'm enjoying myself too," she said.

"How are you finding Leavenworth so far?"

She almost told him great but changed her mind. "To be honest," she said, "things didn't start on a great note."

"On a dark and stormy night…"

"Funny you say that." She hesitated, wondering if she wanted to get into the whole Zach thing.

Then she decided why not. Jack was fun, a good listener—and most importantly he wasn't a teacher. She could get some of this stuff off her chest. "It *was* a dark and stormy night when I first arrived," she said. "I was coming in along Highway 2 when I passed this hitchhiker. I'd hitchhiked a bit when I was younger, but I'd never picked up one before. But it was pouring rain, and this guy was out in the middle of nowhere."

"Where on Highway 2?"

"Twenty miles west or so."

"What was he doing out there by himself?"

"That's the thing. I thought maybe his car broke down. That's what he said happened. Well, he said he had a flat. But I don't remember passing any car on the shoulder."

"Was he drunk?"

Katrina raised her eyebrows in surprise. "How did you know?"

"Because the only place out that way open past dinnertime is a strip club. Guess he spent all his cash on booze and strippers and had to walk home."

Katrina contemplated this. It made sense. Zach had been too embarrassed to admit he'd been at a strip club, so he made up the story about getting a flat.

"So you pick him up and he turns out to be drunk?" Jack said.

"Long story short," she said, "he was acting a bit weird, I realized I'd made a mistake, so when he asked me where I was going I told him only to the next turnoff—Lake Wenatchee. I told him I had a cabin there. Do you know it?"

"The lake? Sure. It's beautiful."

"Well, Zach wouldn't get out of the car—that's his name. He asked me to go for a drink and stuff. I told him no."

Jack frowned. "And?"

"It just got really uncomfortable, I sort of freaked out—and he finally got out. But here's the bizarre part. He's a teacher at Cascade High School with me. He teaches philosophy."

"Oh, boy."

"I tried to talk with him. There was this school thing the other day, drinks at a pub. I told him I wanted to, you know, I wanted to put the past behind us. But for whatever reason he didn't want to, and, well, here's the thing, he's been making things…difficult…for me."

Jack frowned. "Difficult?"

Katrina sighed. "I feel silly even talking about this."

"Tell me."

"Zach made this toast in front of all our colleagues—telling them that I had a cabin on the lake and I wanted to have them all there this weekend."

"I hope you told him to go fuck himself—pardon the language."

She was shaking her head. "I should have…"

Jack seemed surprised. "You didn't?"

"You weren't there, Jack. He put me on the spot. I was standing up in front of everyone. What was I supposed to say? 'Sorry, guys, I don't have a cabin, I lied about the whole thing?'"

"You should have told them this vindictive little prick who spent the night stuffing bills down G-strings scared the crap out of you, so you made up the cabin thing to get him out of your car."

"In hindsight, yes, I should have. But at the time… Put yourself in my shoes. I'm the new teacher. Nobody knows me. They know Zach. And on the first day I meet everyone I, what, I accuse him of…I don't know." She shook her head. "Anyway, it doesn't matter anymore. I spoke to my sister yesterday. She's coming to Leavenworth to visit me this weekend. I told Zach this, and I told him to tell everyone there is no party."

"So it's settled?" Jack said.

"Damn better be."

* * *

Outside King Ludwig's, the air was brisk but pleasant. The sodium-vapor streetlamps cast golden pools of light on the sidewalk. A four-horse team trotted up the street, pulling an old-fashioned wagon. The two drivers, dressed in traditional German clothing, waved at Jack and Katrina, who waved back.

"Sometimes this place feels like Disneyland,"

Katrina said.

"It's one of a kind, no question there," Jack said.

She pointed east. "I'm parked that way."

Jack nodded in the other direction. "My hotel's that way. Want a nightcap?"

His words zapped her. "I should get home…"

"It's still early."

"I really should. But how about dinner again? I'm free anytime next week."

"Works for me." He frowned. "Actually, I might be away on business."

She recalled him telling her he was only passing through Leavenworth. "Away as in not coming back?" she asked.

"No, I'll be back. Not sure how long I'll be gone for though."

"What do you do?"

"Isn't this the stuff you're supposed to talk about over a nightcap?"

Katrina hesitated. She knew what a nightcap led to. She should go home—but to what? Bandit and her empty bed? Was she going to remain celibate for the rest of her life?

"How far is the hotel?" she asked.

Jack took her hand and led her to a Victorian stucco-and-timber building called the Blackbird Lodge. He fished the room key out of his pocket and opened the door.

She stepped inside first. The lights were off, though silver moonlight dusted the windows. She heard the door close, then felt Jack's hands on her shoulders. They slid down her arms, slipped around her waist. She turned toward him. They kissed forcefully.

Then they were moving backward into the room, bumping furniture, undressing each other, collapsing onto the bed.

CHAPTER 9

In the faculty lounge, Katrina was retrieving her lunch from the refrigerator when Bob asked her what he should bring tomorrow night.

She turned, an apple in one hand, a ham sandwich in the other. "Sorry?" she said.

"Saturday!" he said, his bearded face jovial as usual. "Beer, obviously. I'm talking about food. Does the cabin have a bar-b-que?"

This set off the other teachers talking about what they were bringing.

"Guys, guys!" Katrina said, hardly believing what she was witnessing. "Didn't Zach tell you?"

"Tell us what?" a woman named Cindy asked.

"That my sister's coming to visit me this weekend."

"Sure!" Bob said in his booming voice. "Can't wait to meet her."

"Meet her?" Katrina said.

"She's going to love the cake I've made," Monica

said. "It's a family recipe."

"I actually—I asked Zach to tell you guys the party was off."

"Off?" Monica said, her face dropping.

"My sister and I...we were just going to spend some quiet time together."

The room went awkwardly quiet.

"What about the email?" Monica said.

"What email?"

"The one Zach sent. We've already paid for the bus."

"Excuse me," Katrina said. Leaving her apple and sandwich on the table, she went searching for Zach's classroom. Her anger—no, her incredulity that he would do something like this—rose with each step, so by the time she'd reached his room she blew in through the door.

Zach looked up from a stack of papers he was correcting.

"What did I tell you yesterday morning, Zach?" she demanded, stopping in front of his desk.

"What are you talking about?" he said.

"Yesterday morning, Zach! I told you my sister was coming this weekend!"

"So?"

"I told you to tell everyone else."

"I did. I told them. I sent an email."

"What was in the email?"

"That your sister was coming this weekend."

"And?"

"She'd be at the party."

"Jesus, Zach!" Katrina wanted to hit him. "I told you my sister was coming, and I told you to tell everyone the party was off."

"No, you told me your sister was coming. You never said anything about canceling the party."

"Yes, I did, Zach."

"I don't remember that."

Katrina clenched her jaw. "Why are you doing this?"

"Doing what?"

She glared at him.

"Listen, Kat," Zach said levelly. "What's the big deal? It's just a party. Trust me, no one cares whether you have furniture or not."

"It's not about furniture."

"Then what's it about?"

"Zach, the party's off."

He held up his hands defensively. "Hey, I'm not getting any more mixed up in this, Kat. I've already told everyone what you asked me to tell them—"

"You didn't!"

"I told them your sister was coming."

"You never told them the party was off."

"Whatever, look, this has nothing to do with me anymore. I'm not going around telling everyone you've changed your mind."

"I haven't changed my mind, Zach, you know that."

"This isn't Seattle, Kat. Teachers here—it's a tight community. They like things like this, get-togethers. They get excited about them. If you want to go tell everyone you're postponing this thing—"

"I'm not *postponing* anything."

"I have work to do—"

"Fuck you, Zach," she said and left.

* * *

As Katrina pulled into Blackbird Lodge, memories from the night before returned to her, temporarily lifting her black mood. She passed through the hotel lobby and knocked on the door to Jack's room. He appeared in the doorway wearing track pants and nothing else. His powerful upper body glistened with sweat. She'd never seen the tattoos on his chest before, not last night because it was too dark, and not this morning because he'd been up and dressed and making coffee before she'd opened her eyes. There were some tribal designs done in the same green ink as on his arms, along with a wolf's head encircled by a dream catcher, and a bald eagle draped in the American flag.

She cleared her throat. "Sorry," she said. "I should have called. I can come back."

"Nonsense!" he said. "I was just finishing my workout. Come in." He directed her to a chair, then pulled on a T-shirt. "So what's up?"

"I just needed someone to talk to."

"Sure."

She picked up where they'd left off at King Ludwig's. "Remember what I told you about that teacher I work with, and the party at the cabin I'm supposed to be having tomorrow night?"

"On Lake Wenatchee."

"Well, it's still on."

Jack raised his eyebrows. "That Zach guy didn't cancel it?"

"Miscommunication, he says."

"You believe him?"

"Not at all. He knows I don't have a cabin. I know he knows. He's just doing this as some sort of...I don't know. Revenge? I could strangle him. I really could."

Jack leaned forward, eyes hard. "Do you know where he lives?"

"No idea."

"What's his last name?"

"Marshall. Why?"

"I'm going to go talk with him. I can be persuasive."

Katrina eyed Jack's strong forearms and hands, and she was sure he could be persuasive; he could twist Zach into a pretzel if he wanted to. "No, Jack. He's just a kid. Besides, this whole thing is my fault. I'm going to straighten it out."

"How?"

"I got a list of faculty phone numbers from the secretary at the school. I'm going to call everyone tonight and tell them the party is off."

"Calling them at their homes, at the eleventh

hour? They're not going to be too happy about that."

"What other choice do I have?"

Jack shrugged. "Why not just rent a cabin?"

She blinked. "Huh?"

"Rent a cabin on the lake for tomorrow night. It's off-season. A lot of people will be leasing. They'll probably want a week commitment, but I bet we could talk someone into one weekend."

Katrina shook her head. "I can't."

"Why not?"

"It's not right."

"Not right?"

"It'd be lying—again."

"No, hold on now," Jack said. "You didn't tell this Zach guy you actually owned a cabin, did you?"

"What do you mean?"

"Did you tell him you owned one, or were renting one?"

"I don't know." She shook her head. "Neither, I think. I just said I had one."

"Well, there you go," Jack said, smiling. "Anyone asks tomorrow, you just tell them you're renting the place—which means, if you rent it right now, you won't really be lying at all."

Katrina frowned, thinking that over. "I don't know…"

"Let's at least have a look."

Jack's hotel room was furnished with knotty pine furniture, a fireplace, a king bed, a kitchenette, and a cabinet holding a large TV.

There was no computer. Jack, however, produced a laptop from a shoulder bag and connected it to the Wi-Fi.

"It's asking for a credit card," he said. "I lost mine last week and haven't gotten the replacement. Got one handy?"

She gave him her VISA. He logged onto the net, then did a quick Google search. Lake Wenatchee was apparently a popular vacation spot, as there were several pages of listings.

Jack clicked a link for a newly renovated alpine villa and read the specs: "Outdoor hot tub, satellite TV, granite counters, cathedral ceilings, dishwasher—"

"No way," Katrina said.

"Sounds pretty good to me."

"I told everyone the cabin didn't even have furniture."

"Tell them you were being modest."

She shook her head. "No, Jack. That one is ridiculous."

"All right." He clicked a different link. "A-frame, true log cabin with loft. Open living/dining room, laundry cubby, one bath. Nearby amenities: horseshoes, mountain biking, rock climbing, fishing—"

"How many bedrooms?"

"Just one. The loft."

"That sounds more like it."

Jack checked the availability. "You want it, it's yours."

"How much does it cost?"

He shook his head. "I talked you into this. It's on me."

"How much, Jack?"

"Weekly rates—$740 to $850. But hold on, yeah, they have nightly rates too. $120 midweek, $150 weekends. So what do you say? You want it?"

Katrina thought of a hundred reasons why she should say no.

"Okay," she told him.

❋ ❋ ❋

Later that night Katrina awoke bathed in sweat. A scream too big for her throat never made it out of her mouth, and all that emerged was a strangled cry. She was breathing hard and fast as she recalled the gruesome images that had been crawling through her head.

It was the same nightmare that had plagued her sleep ever since Shawn had passed away. In it she was chained to a wall and Shawn was suspended from the ceiling of some sort of dungeon. A big wooden door would creak open, a faceless man would appear, and she would be forced to watch as he cut and pulled Shawn apart like a chicken on a cutting board.

Katrina heard the tick-tock of a wall clock, loud in the otherwise silent room.

"You okay?"

Katrina started. She had forgotten she was in Jack's bed. After they'd booked the cabin, she'd called Zach to tell him the directions to it, so he could tell Lance, the bus driver (Zach had been clearly surprised and maybe even disappointed, and she had reveled at the moment). Then Jack had taken her to dinner—this time to a French restaurant—and they'd returned to his hotel where they'd made love a second time.

The blinds were open a crack. In the glossy moonlight she could make out the strong lines that delineated Jack's face. He was propped up on his elbows. He'd taken his ponytail out earlier, and his long hair fell over his shoulders.

"I'm fine," she told him.

"Bad dream?"

"Yes," she admitted.

"What about?"

"I don't want to talk about it."

"You sure?"

"Yes, but thank you—thank you for everything."

Nodding silently, he lay back down, and she lay down next to him, pressing herself against his body, hoping he couldn't feel the tears warming her eyes.

CHAPTER 10

Saturday morning. Katrina was sitting on her front porch, drinking a freshly brewed cup of coffee, trying not to think too much about the evening's upcoming event. She watched a yellow warbler foraging on her lawn for a while. Then she finished the coffee, went back inside, and rinsed the mug in the kitchen sink. She was trying to decide whether she was hungry or not when a car horn honked outside. She returned to the living room and looked through the window. A sleek beetle-black Porsche was parked behind her Honda. It had a swoopy nose, those distinctive headlamps, and a rear spoiler. She'd noticed the same car parked out front of the Blackbird Lodge yesterday, but hadn't suspected it belonged to Jack.

The driver's door opened and Jack stepped out, dressed in chinos, a white linen shirt beneath a cream-colored cardigan, and brown boat shoes a shade lighter than his belt. He looked like he'd just stepped off a yacht docked in Monte Carlo.

Katrina rubbed the top of Bandit's head. He was lying in the middle of the floor, sulking. When he'd noticed her packing earlier, he'd worked himself into a frenzied excitement, assuming they were going on another road trip together. When he didn't see his leash go into the suitcase, his energy dissipated, and he began making whining noises.

"I'm only going to be gone for one night, bud," she told him. "You got all the food and water you need in your bowls. But no chewing the furniture." That was a bad habit of his, a way of letting her know he was not happy being left on his own.

She touched her nose to his snout. He gave her cheek a halfhearted lick.

"That's a good boy."

She retrieved her suitcase from the atrium and stepped out the front door. Jack was now on the porch, leaning against the banister. Seeing him, she felt a flutter of excitement in her chest. She knew she was falling for him, and she knew that was a bad idea, given he could pick up and leave town any day. Yet she couldn't help it. This morning it had taken her three changes of clothes until she'd decided on her present outfit, a butterfly-print dress and matching butterfly jewelry.

Jack complimented her dress, carried her small overnight bag to the Porsche's trunk, then opened the door for her. He got in behind the wheel, slipped on a pair of Ray-Bans, then turned down her street. He kept to the speed limit as they passed the Howard Johnson and Best Western and all the other hotels positioned at the westernmost point of the town, but as soon as they passed Icicle Road and there was nothing around them except hills and trees, he opened up the throttle.

The morning was chilly and blue, the sun a gold coin burning brightly in the east. The countryside was sprayed with a fiery blast of autumn colors: a field of orange huckleberry bushes, mustard-yellow alpine larches and aspen, deep-red vine maple. The towering sugar-peaked mountains remained rooted in the background, unmoving, millennium-old monoliths seemingly impervious to human concepts of time and speed.

"You know," she said, "we never had that nightcap talk about what you do."

"I'm between jobs right now." He overtook a green sedan.

"Before?" she asked.

"Used to own a small gym. A ring, some punching bags, weights. Then I got lucky with some investments."

Katrina was slightly disappointed by this revelation. Jack had been an enigma to her: uniquely handsome, charismatic, mysterious. She didn't know what she'd expected his profession to be, but retired and sitting on a nest egg seemed anticlimactic.

"So you owned a gym," she said. "Does that mean you know how to box?"

He glanced at her, and she could see a tiny

version of herself reflected in his mirrored lenses. "Box, sure—though I'm probably a bit rusty these days. I started with karate when I was a kid, then got into judo, then kickboxing and boxing."

"So you used to…like…compete or something?"

"For a few years."

"Wow," she said, genuinely surprised. He had the physique to be a fighter, but he seemed too refined, too articulate, to have spent his days in a ring trading blows to the body and head.

He asked her, "What about you? Always been a teacher?"

She nodded. "My father pressured me into going to teachers college. He was all about stability, security."

"But you like kids?"

"Oh, yes, definitely. Don't get me wrong. I might not have chosen to get into teaching had it been up to me, but I like the job, and I like the students— well, most of them. Where are you from?"

He glanced at her again. "As in where was I born?"

"Born, grew up, yes."

"I was born in Colorado. My mom was Ojibwa. My dad's side of the family was here since George Washington. Mom stayed at home raising me. Dad was a lumberjack. Then I got pretty sick— leukemia—and had to go to the hospital. I spent months in the kids' ward with all the other kids who were supposed to die. Moms were always there crying, dads trying not to. Looking back, it was pure grief. That's the only way to describe it, I guess. Grief—grief everywhere. Most of the friends I made ended up dead."

"God, Jack," she said. "But you made it."

"Yeah, one of the few in the ward who survived. But home wasn't any better. My dad was a bad drunk. He was beating up my mom all the time, beating me up too. That's why I got into karate —can you believe that? Get into karate to protect your mom from your dad."

"How old were you?"

"Nine or ten. I still got my ass whipped by him until I turned fourteen or so. He came home one night and went after my mom for some stupid thing or another. Started hitting her until she was curled up on the sofa, screaming at him to stop. I —" He hesitated. "Let's just say my dad left and never came back. That was the last my mom or I saw of him. I kept going to the gym though. The judo and kickboxing—I was into it all. Ended up dropping out of high school to work for the guy who owned the gym. He was an old fellow. Heart of gold but no business sense. The gym was going under, and I sort of helped him turn it around. We eventually became partners, then I bought him out, made some investments." He shrugged. "And here we are."

Katrina was quiet for a moment, absorbing what he'd told her. "I'm sorry, Jack," she said. "For what you went through."

"That's life," he said. "You live, you learn, you

grow. I wouldn't be who I am today if I didn't go through all that shit as a kid. And I likely wouldn't be cruising down this highway on this lovely morning with a lovely passenger beside me had things been any different." He winked at her.

She couldn't help but laugh—and blush. "You're something, Jack."

"You are too, Kat," he said. "I mean it. I haven't met many women like you."

She wanted to ask him about that—his past relationships. But she felt as though she'd already pried too much for one morning, and instead she said, "Why Leavenworth? You mentioned you were passing through. But why here? I mean, it's beautiful and everything, but it's not exactly..."

"I don't know. Maybe it's just what you said. It's beautiful. It seemed like a nice place to spend a few weeks."

A few weeks, she thought—trying not to think about that. She looked out her window at the colorful scenery, and they fell silent for a spell.

When they reached a sign announcing the turnoff to State Route 207, Katrina flashed back to the night in her car with Zach, in the middle of the storm. Had that only been a week ago? It seemed like months.

Jack turned right and followed the smaller highway to Lake Wenatchee State Park, where they ended up on rutted back roads, which were not made for low-riding sports cars. Eventually they pulled up to the A-frame log cabin she'd rented. It was in a little disrepair, weathered by the elements, but exactly what she'd wanted.

Jack pulled up beside a silver pickup truck parked out front, and they got out of the Porsche. Katrina breathed in the fresh mountain air.

An elderly man dressed in black cords and a black turtleneck and leaning on a polished cane limped out the front door. His thinning gray hair was cut close to the scalp, his skin dotted with liver spots. He peered at them through rimless eyeglasses. "You made it," he announced, then broke into a coughing fit.

"I'm Jack," Jack said, shaking hands. "This is Katrina."

"Howdy," the man said. "I'm Charlie. I don't got much time. Got to get me to a goddamn funeral. Seems like I'm going to more 'n' more of 'em each year. Soon it's gonna be me. Who's gonna come? No one, cause they're all fuckin' dead. But come in, I'll give you the tour. Don't mind your shoes."

The interior of the cabin was plain and rustic. A wagon-wheel chandelier hung from the ceiling. A patched sofa and rocking chair faced an old stone fireplace. The kitchen contained the bare necessities: scarred fridge, ancient stove, stainless-steel sink, and two sets of cupboards. Katrina poked her head in the bathroom and discovered a flimsy-looking plastic toilet, a sink below a mirror, and an old-fashioned, claw-footed tub, which made her think momentarily of her bathroom back in Leavenworth, and the creep who'd been looking in.

A narrow flight of dangerously steep steps led to the second-floor loft, which was crammed with a queen bed and a small night table on which sat a blinking alarm clock. The smell of old wood and old blankets hung over everything, musty but not unpleasant.

"This place has been in the family for years," Charlie told them. "Grandpa built it after the Depression. I came up here all the time as a kid. Got no brothers or sisters, so my parents left it to me—the only thing they left me worth two shits, mind you." He whipped out a handkerchief to smother a coughing fit that left him looking shaky. "Fuckin' cold," he said. "Reason I'm renting. We live in Skykomish. The missus don't want me out here in the fall or winter. No insulation, no central heating. She thinks I'll get pneumonia. Get yourself pneumonia, she says, and you best go sleep in your grave 'cause you'll be dead soon enough. Goddamn women. Can't stand 'em. No offense, ma'am."

Katrina merely smiled, then handed him the one hundred and fifty she'd withdrawn from the ATM the night before.

Charlie counted it, then frowned. "Didn't I mention the deposit?"

"What deposit?" Jack asked.

"Hell if I didn't," Charlie said, scratching his bald head. "Can't trust my memory no more. I need another hundred deposit. Never used to ask, but last year I rented the place out to two college kids over Memorial Day weekend. Said they just wanted to do some fishin', hikin'. I don't care, I said, just as long as I get my money. You know what they ended up doin'? Havin' a big old party. Twenty friends, I reckon. Helluva mess. Goddamn beer spilled over the floor, cigarette butts everywhere you looked, bottles behind every rock 'n' tree. Probably pissed all over my trees too, I bet. Kids nowadays got no damn respect for nothing. Thank the Lord they didn't burn the cabin down. But I learned my lesson, I'll tell you that. Don't rent to no snot-nosed kids no more. That's why all the questions last night."

"So no parties, huh?" Jack said lightly.

"Hell, no! But you look like a respectable fella, am I right?"

"All we have in mind is a quiet weekend." Jack took two fifties from his wallet and gave them to the old man. "One hundred for the deposit."

Charlie took the money and stuffed it in his pocket. He gave them a final, lengthy appraisal before handing over a single key and bidding farewell. Then he limped down to his pickup truck, hiked himself inside, and drove off with a toot of the horn.

"Why'd you do that?" Katrina said to Jack as they watched the truck disappear into the trees.

He looked at her. "Do what?"

"Tell him it's just us here? We should have told him we're having some friends over."

"You heard him talk. He's a crazy bastard. He might have told us to go to hell. Besides, what does it matter? He's never going to know if we have people over or not."

Katrina knew Jack was right. Nevertheless, a premonition stole over her, sending a chill down her spine. She turned into a circle, eyeing the property.

"It's no big deal," Jack said.

"I don't like it, that's all."

"What's not to like? Look around. Smell the air."

"It's just another lie," she said, and she almost wanted to laugh. She felt like someone waist-deep in quicksand. The more she struggled to free herself, the deeper she sank.

"You're worrying too much," Jack told her, taking her hand. "Everything is going to be fine."

CHAPTER 11

It was 7:30 p.m. and the sun was dipping behind the mountains in the west, throwing long, scarlet streaks across the sky. The yellow school bus bumped and chugged its way down a back road bordered by towering aspen and moss-covered maple trees. Inside it the atmosphere was upbeat and expectant. The female teachers were lumped up by Lance, gossiping and chatting. Dolly had a guitar and sometimes she would strum a few chords and get everyone singing. The male teachers were grouped in the middle of the bus, cracking jokes and popping beer cans. Currently Bob was telling an ice-fishing story that ended with him falling through the ice.

Zach was sitting at the back of the bus, watching all this with a combination of contempt and envy. It was the feeling you got when you were looking at something from the outside in. He didn't fit in with the other teachers, didn't really want to, but nevertheless felt a sense of missing out. He would have felt better had the missing out been his decision, not theirs. But whatever.

He cracked open his sixth Beck's and took a swallow. He'd had four before he left his house—no way was he getting on a bus with thirty people stone sober; he'd have one of his panic attacks inside of five minutes—and then two more since, including the one he'd just opened.

He thought again about the phone conversation with Katrina the previous evening. He'd been giving her a hard time all week because she'd kicked him out of her car. But now it seemed she'd done that not because she thought he was a weirdo or loser or something along those lines but because she really did have a cabin on Lake Wenatchee—which made him feel not only embarrassed by his behavior but like a real shithead too. He'd considered not coming tonight, but decided to in the end. It was time to maybe apologize to her, let bygones be bygones, or whatever they say.

Maybe they could even become friends...maybe more than friends. She was attractive. He'd always thought that. And maybe that was part of the reason he'd been giving her such a hard time.

He closed his eyes, picturing her as she'd been in the bathtub, her breasts when she'd reached for the wine, her butt when she stood...

A noise disrupted these images. In the middle of the bus, Graham Douglas was making his way down the aisle toward the back. He was grabbing each seat for balance, resembling someone wading through waist-deep water. He took the seat across from Zach, leaned forward, unzipped his pants, and pissed into an empty beer bottle. "There's no toilet on this thing, man," he said to Zach without looking at him. "What the fuck do they expect you to do? Piss out the window?" He did up his pants, stuffed the full bottle in the crack where the seat met the side of the bus, then reached across the aisle and snagged one of Zach's beers.

Graham was one of the more popular teachers at the school. He sang in some garage band that played the occasional gig around the state. He was older than Zach, maybe twenty-six or seven, and with his red afro, mustache, and muttonchops he was one of the ugliest motherfuckers Zach knew. He dressed like he was from the seventies as well, with tie-dye shirts and bell bottoms. He twisted the cap off the beer, took a swig, and said, "How dope is tonight going to be, Zachy-boy? Bob-o brought a couple of fishing rods. See if we can't catch some pike. You fish, Zachy-boy?"

Zach shrugged. He hated that nickname. It was a dig at him, a condescending reminder he was the youngest teacher at the school.

"What's wrong, Zachy-boy?" Graham said. "Cat caught your tongue? By the way, why the hell are you sitting way back here by yourself? We're missing your deep philosophy shit. Seriously. You're a whack kid, you know that? Who else knows so much about the next stage of evolution, right?"

At a party the year before, Zach had gotten pretty drunk and ended up in a discussion about evolution with Henry Lee, a science teacher at the school. Zach had gone on about head transplants and cyborgs and immortality and all that shit. Graham and some of the other teachers had mocked him about it for months.

"Fuck off, Graham," he said.

"Whoa, man! What's up with you? I'm telling you the real deal. We're missing you up there. Hey, is she single?"

"Who?"

"The new teacher."

"Why would I know?"

Graham grinned, patted Zach on the shoulder, then headed back to join Bob and the others in the center of the bus.

Zach watched him go, and all of a sudden he felt queasy and lightheaded. His eyes started to water and blur. He groped at the window and yanked down the upper pane of glass, letting in a sharp gust of wind. He breathed deeply and steadily, counting to ten, then twenty. He began to feel better again. He looked up the aisle. Thankfully no one had noticed. They didn't know he had panic attacks. They would have assumed he'd drunk himself retarded before the party even started.

A short time later the bus shuddered to a halt. This was accompanied by a rising buzz of excited chatter. Zach peered through the window. A small log cabin was ahead of them, facing the shadowy expanse of the lake. He grabbed his six-pack of beer, which now only had three remaining in it, and his backpack, which held his harder booze, then followed the noisy procession off the bus. He started toward the cabin but stopped abruptly when the cabin's front door opened and Katrina appeared to greet everyone—along with some muscled dude with long hair and a big smile.

CHAPTER 12

The teachers entered the cabin in a wave, stuffing the fridge with beer and mixers and laying out snacks and other food on the kitchen table. Someone turned up the stereo, so that along with all the chatter you soon couldn't hear yourself speak. Jack, it seemed, had no problem socializing with a roomful of strangers. In fact, with his hearty greetings and easygoing charm, his ability to work the room and make everyone feel welcome, he quickly became the center of attention.

Katrina stood with Crystal, who'd just returned from the kitchen with two Bloody Marys. Like Katrina, Crystal had blonde hair and blue eyes, though due to her extra weight, her face was a bit pudgier, her cheeks fuller.

Katrina sipped the drink. "Not bad," she said. "I hope you're not going to drop out of college and take up bartending?"

"No," Crystal said. "But it doesn't sound like a

bad idea."

"College is supposed to be fun. Give it a chance."

"Yeah, yeah, we'll see. So where's this Zach the Maniac anyway?"

Katrina had been wondering that herself. She looked around the room and spotted Zach in the corner, by himself.

Crystal was squinting in the same direction. She was nearsighted and refused to wear glasses or contact lenses. "You didn't tell me he was so good-looking."

"He's not," Katrina said flatly.

"Yeah, he is."

"Don't even think about it, Chris. Actually, I need to have a word with him. I'll be back."

"Can I come?"

"I'm serious, Chris. Stay away from him."

Crystal seemed as if she was about to protest, but then she shrugged. Katrina went over to Zach. He was wearing jeans and a long-sleeved shirt, drinking a beer. His eyes were glassy, the way they'd been back on the highway.

"Hi, Zach," she said.

"Who's the Indian?"

She blinked. "Excuse me?"

"Looks like he just escaped from jail."

"His name is Jack."

"Looks like he rapes boys."

"Jesus, Zach," she said. "I thought we could have a normal conversation for once."

"Are you dating him?"

"Who?"

"The Indian."

"His name's Jack, Zach."

"Are you dating him?"

"What does that matter?"

"Are you dating him?"

"It's not your business—"

"Fuck you," he said. "And fuck that Indian too." He stepped past her.

She seized his shoulder, baffled by his behavior. "Zach—"

He turned, rolling his shoulder as if her fingers were acid. "Don't fucking touch me!" he snapped. Those nearby them went quiet. Oblivious to this, Zach went on just as loudly, "Where the fuck is he anyway? Outside smoking a pipe? Doing a rain dance?"

Jack appeared a moment later. He glanced at Katrina, then at Zach.

"Problem here?" he asked.

"Fuck you, chief," Zach said.

"I'm guessing you're Zach."

"Why are you guessing that?"

"Because you're the only asshole in the room."

"Jack—" Katrina said.

Before she could finish her sentence, however, Zach swung the beer bottle in his hand, beer spraying in an arc. Jack caught Zach's wrist and twisted it sharply. Zach grunted and dropped the bottle, which shattered against the floor. Jack slipped his arm beneath Zach's armpit and grabbed a fistful of his shaggy hair. "Time to go, friend," he said.

"Get your motherfucking hands off me!"

"Jack," Katrina said. "Let him go."

But Jack was already shoving Zach roughly forward, toward the front door, like a bouncer escorting a drunk from the club. Zach continued to spew off more curses, but he couldn't free himself. Then they were outside. The door slapped the frame with a loud, flat crack. Silence hung in the air until someone snickered.

It was Graham. "That frog is so fucked it isn't funny," he said.

Katrina hurried after Jack and Zach. As soon as she stepped outside, the voices inside rose into a swell of chatter.

Jack was standing at the bottom of the porch steps. Past him Katrina could make out the silhouette of Zach as he stumbled in the direction of the school bus. She started to follow him, but Jack touched her arm.

"Leave him," he said.

"I need to talk to him."

"He needs to sober up. What was that about anyway?"

She shook her head. "I think he's jealous of you."

"Of me?" Jack seemed surprised. "You mean he likes you?"

"I don't know."

"I thought he was your archenemy or something."

"I guess things are more complicated than that."

"So that's the reason he's been such a prick to you? You weren't reciprocating his feelings?"

"I really don't know. But I feel bad about what just happened. I think I should talk to him."

"Later," Jack said, taking her hand in his. "As I said, he needs to sober up. And you're missing your own party."

CHAPTER 13

C rystal Burton was sitting in a sling chair on the dock, drinking a Seagram's Cooler, and listening to the lap of the waves against the shore. Across the lake pinpricks of light floated in the darkness, which she assumed to be from other cabins, or maybe a campground or two. To the west, a rocky point prickling with trees blocked her view, but along the eastern shore she could make out the shadowy form of another dock jutting out over the water. She could also see the outline of the corresponding cabin.

She sipped the cooler and thought about what had happened earlier. She felt bad for Zach. After Jack had taken him outside, everyone had starting laughing at him, calling him a drunk and other names. Crystal left, not wanting to hear it. She could relate to not fitting in. She wasn't like Kat, pretty and outgoing. She was the ugly sister, the introvert. It wasn't like they were ever competitive or anything—Kat was ten years older—but Crystal nevertheless felt as though she'd always lived in the shadow of her sister. Then when their parents died—well, that didn't do anything to improve her self-confidence. She ended up spending more and more time on her own, in her room, watching movies and eating too much. She hated herself for it, but she couldn't help it. And now college... it was like a permanent audition to be cool. She'd only been on campus a couple of days, and already everyone seemed to have made friends except for her.

Crystal sipped her drink and noticed someone sitting on the adjacent dock. She took her eyeglasses from her pocket—she avoided wearing them because they made her look more bookish than she already was—and slipped them on.

She still couldn't make out who it was. It was too dark. Yet she didn't think it was the neighbor. Someone from the party? But why would they go way over there—?

Zach, she realized.

Crystal returned to the cabin. In the kitchen she opened the Eskimo cooler and took the last cooler from the four-pack she'd brought. She also snagged one of the numerous beers that were floating in the cold water.

Back outside, she didn't return to the sling chair but went east, toward where the school bus was parked. The night thickened around her as she left the light from the porch. She entered a copse of trees that blocked out most of the sky, so it was nearly completely black. She slowed so she didn't trip or fall. She assumed if she went far enough along the road, staying parallel to the lake, she would come to the neighboring dock.

It turned out she was right. Fifty yards on the trees thinned, and she could once again see the flat expanse of the lake and the neighbor's dock. This close she could make out the person she'd spotted earlier. She'd been right. It was Zach.

She followed a worn path down a rocky slope to the dock. Twigs snapped beneath her footfalls and small pebbles rolled into the water.

Zach heard her approach and turned around.

"My name's Crystal. Hi." She stopped next to him.

"Sorry," he said, starting to stand. "I didn't think anyone was home."

She shook her head. "This isn't my place. I'm Katrina's sister. I came with her earlier."

Even in the poor light, she could see the surprise on his face. "You're her sister?" His voice hardened. "Did she send you here to talk to me?"

"No. I was on the other dock and saw you."

"What were you doing on the dock?"

"Just hanging out."

"By yourself?"

"You're hanging out by yourself."

"So what do you want?"

She frowned. "Well, nothing. I was just bored." She held forth the beer she'd taken from the cooler. "Brought this for you."

He raised a half-full bottle of whiskey.

"Oh—well, okay," she said. "I guess I'll go. Sorry to bother you."

"No, wait." He cleared his throat. "I'm sorry. I was just surprised you're Katrina's sister, that's all. I didn't even know she had one." He gestured for her to sit. "Stay if you want."

She studied him for a moment, then sat.

"Hey, how old are you?" she asked. "You seem pretty young to be a teacher."

Zach grunted. "So I've been told. What about you?"

"I'm a student."

"I mean, how old are you?"

"Nineteen."

"That's a big age difference, you and your sister."

"I guess I was an accident."

Zach chuckled.

Crystal took a pack of Marlboros from her handbag and offered him one.

"I don't smoke," he said.

She lit up. "I started last year to lose weight."

He chuckled again.

"So you teach philosophy?" she said.

"Ancient and modern, yeah."

"Who's your favorite philosopher?"

He shrugged. "Aristotle, probably."

"Why?"

"I don't know. But he's probably done more for humanity than any other single person."

"Good reason, I guess. I like Thales. Philosophy's my minor."

"Seriously?"

They ended up talking about philosophy for a bit longer, then lighter stuff, like movies and books. The time passed quickly. Crystal finished the cooler, then began sharing the bottle of whiskey with Zach. She never drank hard liquor, and it hit her quickly. But she didn't want to stop. She was having a good time. She couldn't understand why Katrina despised Zach so much— or why everyone seemed to, for that matter.

At one point the party spilled out of the cabin and down to the dock next to the one they were on. Voices and laughter floated across the water. Someone brought a portable stereo and cranked up the music.

Zach finished the whiskey and was about to get up.

"Where are you going?" she asked him, her head spinning.

"I have more booze in the bus."

"You just drank an entire bottle of whiskey."

"You helped."

"I mean—it's a lot. Sorry, I don't want to lecture…"

He considered that. "Do you have any phobias?"

"Like a fear of heights or something?"

"Yeah, like that."

"I don't like spiders."

"Arachnophobia."

"Yeah... Also, and don't laugh, but I don't like clowns."

"Coulrophobia."

"You're making that up!"

He shook his head. "I'm a bit of an expert on phobias. Ever hear of agoraphobia?"

"Fear of going outside?"

"Close enough."

"So what about it?"

"That's what I have."

"Agoraphobia?"

"Yeah."

She thought he was kidding and said so.

"Places I'm familiar with," he explained, "I'm fine. My house, the school. But sometimes when I'm somewhere not familiar—I get these panic attacks."

"What kind of panic attacks?"

"You know—panic attacks."

"But you're fine now?"

He held up the empty whiskey bottle. "Takes the edge off."

"So that's why you drink so much—?" Crystal cut herself off. "Sorry," she added quickly. "I didn't mean it like that. I just meant—"

But then Zach was leaning close to her, and they were kissing. She was both thrilled and terrified. They kissed lightly for a bit, then harder, more passionately. This was her first real kiss, and she couldn't believe it was happening.

Zach's hand brushed through her hair. It felt

good. His hand slipped down her cheek, down her neck, and cupped her left breast. That felt even better.

Suddenly Zach broke apart, looking toward the road. "Who the hell's that?"

Crystal blinked, a little fuzzy. Then she heard it too—the approach of a car engine.

Who cares! she wanted to say. We were kissing! But what she said was, "Someone who lives down the road?"

"Isn't your cabin the last one on this road?"

"My cabin?"

"Whatever. Your sister's."

"It's not her—" She cut herself off again.

Zach frowned. "Not her what?"

"Nothing."

"Not her cabin?"

"No, it is. She rents it."

His frown deepened.

"It's true," she insisted.

The sound of the car grew louder. The high beams illuminated the nearby trees, turning them a ghostly gray. They both watched as the car—a light-colored pickup truck—passed by.

Zach got to his feet. "I'll be back in a minute."

"Where are you going?"

"To check it out."

"Why? Who cares?"

But he was already leaving the dock.

CHAPTER 14

Katrina and Jack both heard the vehicle approach. They looked at one other, confused.

Jack went to the window.

"Who is it?" Katrina asked.

"You're not going to like this." He paused. "Charlie's back."

Charlie? Old man Charlie? No-party Charlie? "God!" she exclaimed. She jumped off the sofa —where she and Jack had been sitting, knees touching, drinking wine—and joined Jack at the window. "What's he doing here?"

"I'll go find out."

Jack went to the porch. Katrina followed. Charlie slammed the truck door closed and limped, scowling, toward them. "You!" he spat, stopping at the bottom of the porch steps and waving his cane at Jack. "What did I tell you about havin' no goddamn parties?"

"A few people stopped by," Jack said evenly as

the old man clumped up the steps. "They're all teachers from Cascade High School. Responsible folks. You have nothing to worry about. The place will be as good as new tomorrow morning."

Charlie pointed his cane toward the shouting and music coming from the lake. "Responsible folks, you say? That don't sound like responsible folks to me. Sounds like a wagonload of college bastards. That's what the neighbors said. Ron calls me up and says, 'What the bloody hell is goin' on, Charlie? There's a roaring bender goin' full blast over at your place.' And he lives three cottages down, so I know whatever the fuck a bender is, it's somethin' loud enough to wake the dead, God rest 'em. Outta my way!"

Charlie whacked his cane at Jack's shins, then lurched past like a pirate walking with a peg leg. He shoved open the door and entered the cabin. Katrina and Jack followed. Looking around, Katrina wished she'd had time to clean up. Glasses and beer bottles were left haphazardly on most available surfaces, along with paper plates stacked with leftover food. The kitchen table was a mess. A pile of CDs was fanned out on the floor, next to a box of vinyl records someone had found and rifled through. A maze of dusty footprints led every which way. But it was the spot where Zach had broken his beer bottle that seemed to centerpiece the room. They'd picked up the larger pieces of glass and swept up the smaller shards, then they'd soaked the beer out of the floor with a damp cloth.

Katrina thought it would be fine in the morning, but at the moment the big dark puddle-shaped stain did not look fine at all. It looked like someone had urinated on the center of the floor.

"Mother of all hell!" Charlie said. "You've turned this place into a fuckin' pigpen!" He whirled on them. "I want you and all them friends of yours outta here."

Katrina said, "Hold on, Charlie—"

"Hold on? Hold on? I ain't holdin' on to nothing. And don't you even think about askin' for your deposit back, sugar tits—"

Jack seized Charlie by the shoulder, pressing down on some pressure point. The old man cackled and bent sideways.

"Watch it, pal," Jack said.

"Jack!" Katrina said, surprised. "Let him go!"

Jack released his grip. Charlie stumbled free, bringing his hand up to massage his shoulder. "That's assault, you son of a bitch!" he gasped. "And don't think I ain't gonna report it. I am. Lock your ass up in the slammer. You'll probably like that, won't you, you big ape? Trade this bitch in for—"

This time Jack had Charlie by the throat. He marched him toward the front door, keeping him at arm's length like he was a leaky bag of garbage. The old man tripped over his own feet as he was shoved backward. He swung his cane wildly, hitting Jack a couple of times, but Jack didn't seem to notice.

"Jack!" Katrina said.

"Stay here," he told her over his shoulder. "Won't be a minute."

Charlie gurgled something unintelligible.

"Forget it, Jack, leave him," she said. "It doesn't matter. I'll go tell everyone to leave."

"Stay here," he repeated, disappearing with Charlie outside, the door closing behind them.

Katrina brought her hands to her mouth, forming a steeple. She considered following them outside, but she decided to start cleaning up instead. Maybe if she made the place presentable, and promised to turn down the music, Charlie might reconsider and let them stay after all.

CHAPTER 15

Jack strong-armed Charlie down the porch step to the silver pickup truck. Charlie's eyes were wide and feral, showing something between fury and fear. When Jack figured he was far enough away from the cabin that Katrina couldn't overhear him, he released his grip. Charlie doubled over, rubbed his throat, and tried to catch his sputtering breath. Jack grabbed him by the collar of his shirt and tugged him upright, so he could make eye contact. "I've been easy on you so far because of my friend inside," he said in a quiet voice. "But it's just you and me now, and if I hear anything I don't like, I'm going to hurt you. Bad. Got that?"

Charlie glowered and rubbed his neck and didn't say anything.

"Now, first things first, nobody's going anywhere," Jack went on. "That just isn't happening. So what we're going to do, we're going to walk over to my car. I'm going to get my wallet, and I'm going to give you an extra two hundred dollars for your trouble of coming all the way out here, and then you're going to get into that nice Ford F-150 of yours, and you're going to drive back home, and you're going to enjoy the rest of your evening while we enjoy ours. I'll talk to the teachers on the dock, tell them to keep it down. And tomorrow I'll personally see to it that this place is as new as it can be. Now what do you say, friend? Do we have ourselves a deal?"

For a moment Charlie seemed as if he was about to say something nasty, but then he nodded. Relieved, Jack led him toward the Porsche, opened the sports car's front door, popped the glove compartment, and took out his wallet. As he was twisting out of the car, the old man's cane came slicing through the air. Pain exploded across his face in firecrackers of light. He staggered to one knee. The cane came again. This time down on the back of his skull. He dropped to his side.

"This ain't about no money, you goddamn monkey," Charlie was saying, though the old man's voice seemed to be coming from a place far away. "It's about respect. But I do believe I deserve somethin' for haulin' ass out here. Holy Jesus! I'd say five hundred just about covers it. Now, I'm going to go tell all your no-class friends to get off my fuckin' property. And maybe, if you're lucky, one of 'em will help you get your sorry ass together."

Bolts of pain throbbed behind Jack's face. He

could taste coppery blood mixed with dirt. He brought a hand to the back of his head and felt a walnut-sized lump.

Anger burned inside him, burned away the blackness. He opened his eyes and saw he was facedown in the mud. He pushed himself to his feet, almost toppled over, didn't. His vision was swimming, but he could see enough to make out Charlie, twenty feet away, heading toward the dock.

Jack started after him. With each step some of his strength returned, and he got to within a few feet of Charlie before the old fuck heard him and turned.

"Oh shit no—"

Jack's hand shot forward, fist open. The heel of his palm smashed Charlie's nose, shutting him up midsentence. Cartilage crunched, making a popping sound like knuckles cracking. Blood spurted. Charlie lumbered backward, lost his balance, and landed on his back. Jack kicked the old fuck as hard as he could in the ribs, breaking a whole bunch of them. He kicked him again and again until the rib cage became soft and mushy.

Charlie was moaning, spitting up mouthfuls of blood. One of the moans might have been a word, maybe a plea. Jack didn't know, didn't care. He was seeing red and kept kicking long after Charlie had ceased twitching.

When Jack finally got hold of himself, he stared down at the broken, bloody mess frosted with moonlight.

The gravity of what he'd done sank in, and he felt for a pulse.

Charlie was dead.

Jack swore to himself. Then he swore again, louder. He looked to the cabin and half-expected Katrina to be standing on the porch, watching him in horror. She wasn't. He turned toward the dock. No one had come up. No one had seen what he'd done.

He heard something, leaf litter crackling. He snapped his head in the direction of the noise. The road disappeared into a copse of trees. All was quiet.

"Hello?" he said.

The only answer was the whistle of a breeze and the shiver of leaves.

Jack returned his attention to Charlie. He grabbed the corpse by the scarecrow-like ankles and dragged it into the nearest bushes.

CHAPTER 16

Katrina finished sweeping the floor, thinking the place looked respectable, almost how it had been earlier in the afternoon, minus the dark beer stain on the hardwood. Nevertheless, there was nothing to be done about that except to let it dry on its own.

She set the broom aside just as the door opened and Jack entered. She froze in shock. His nose, mouth, and chin were dripping with blood. Crimson splotches stained his cashmere cardigan.

"Jack!" she said. "What happened?"

He brushed past her and grabbed a bottle of bourbon off the kitchen table. He filled half a tumbler and knocked it back in a single mouthful. "Charlie," he said.

"Charlie? What are you talking about?"

"I tried to pay him off. Offered him two hundred bucks to go home. I went to the car to get my wallet. I was turning around, getting out, when—bam. The fucker whacked me with his cane in the face. Then he whacked me again, on the back of the head."

Katrina was dumbstruck. Then some brain cells kicked in. "You need to go to the hospital. Dammit, where's my phone?"

She started to turn away when he seized her wrist. "You're not calling anyone."

"Don't be ridiculous, Jack. Look at you! Your nose is likely broken."

"Just fetch me my bag from the laundry."

Jack went to the bathroom to clean up. Katrina didn't move, a dozen questions pin-balling inside her head. She considered ordering Jack to go to the hospital with her, but she knew that would be futile. He would do what he wanted to do.

Cursing, she hurried to the laundry and retrieved the black overnight bag Jack had brought with him. She set it on the middle of the living room floor and was unzipping it when the front door clattered open and Graham Douglas strolled in. At the same time, Jack emerged from the bathroom, bare-chested. He'd washed his face and looked better than he had before, but his nose was still a mess, leaking a rivulet of blood.

"Jesus!" Graham exclaimed. "What the hell happened to you, dude?"

Jack shrugged impatiently. "Ran into a tree in the dark."

Graham seemed about to laugh but thought better of it when he saw the look in Jack's eyes. Jack took the white shirt Katrina was holding in her hand, then disappeared back inside the bathroom.

"Some tree," Graham said as he crossed the room to the fridge. The smell of marijuana trailed behind him, skunk-like. He stuffed two beers in his pockets and opened a third. "I thought your sister was in here with you?"

"Chris?" Katrina said. "She's not at the dock with you guys?"

"Nope. By the way, whose truck is that outside?"

Charlie's pickup? Katrina wondered. Had he stuck around? After beating the crap out of Jack? No way. Not unless he was crazy—or unless he hadn't had a chance to leave.

Her blood turned cold.

Feeling Graham's eyes on her, she zipped up the bag and stood. "One of Jack's friends stopped by," she said lightly.

"Where is he?"

"Around somewhere. Out back, maybe."

"Oh—I was supposed to ask when the bus is leaving?"

Katrina checked her watch. It was nine-thirty. "Eleven, I think. Lance is probably sleeping inside it right now if you want to ask him. Or you can confirm with Zach. He organized everything."

"Yeah, I'll do that," he said, heading toward the door. "Keep your cool on—and tell Jack-o to watch out for any more trees."

Katrina hurried to the bathroom door. "Jack?" she said. "Charlie's truck is still here. Why hasn't he left? Where is he?"

The door opened. Jack was wearing the shirt she'd given him. He'd plugged his nostrils with toilet paper and he really did look like a boxer right then—a boxer who had just gone twelve rounds with the defending champ.

"Where did Charlie go?" she pressed. "If he talks to—"

"He's dead," Jack said.

She blinked. "He's what?"

"Dead."

"What are you talking about?"

"It was an accident."

"This isn't funny, Jack."

But he wasn't smiling, and Katrina knew it was true. She must have gone into shock because the next thing she knew she was no longer by the bathroom but sitting next to Jack on the sofa.

She felt as if she were in a dream. Charlie was dead. Dead. The word didn't even seem real. It seemed connected to an abstract idea, not a concrete thing, not a person. Not Charlie.

It didn't make sense. Nothing was making sense.

For a moment she thought she was going to be sick, but the sour sensation passed. A flurry of fresh questions wanted to leap out of her mouth, but only one made it. "How?" she asked.

Jack shrugged. "As I said, he bashed me with his cane. He was heading to the dock to tell everyone to leave. I came around and caught up and hit him. I didn't mean to hit him so hard. But he'd just played baseball with my head, and I wasn't thinking too straight."

Katrina dropped her face into her hands. She couldn't accept they were talking about this. You had conversations about the weather and your job and your friends. You didn't have a conversation about how you killed someone.

"Where's his body?" she asked.

"I moved it to the bushes."

Emotion gave way to reason. She began thinking in terms of cause and effect. "You shouldn't have moved it."

"Someone would have seen it if I hadn't."

"But when the police find it there, they're going to be suspicious—"

"Whoa-ho-ho," Jack said, recoiling from her. "We're not calling the cops."

She stared at him as if he'd spoken another language. "What are you talking about, Jack?"

"I just killed a man, Kat."

"It was an accident. You didn't know one punch was going to kill him. Besides, all they have to do is look at you, your face. It was obviously self-defense."

"Right, Kat. Look at me. I'm six-one, two hundred pounds. Charlie must've been at least seventy. Throw in my fighting background, how's that going to look?"

He was right, she realized. But she also knew they had to call the police. It simply wasn't an option to conceal a murder.

Christ. Was that what it was going to be called? Murder?

Her initial denial was turning into horror.

Jack was going to jail. That was the cold reality of it.

"This is all my fault," she said. "If I hadn't lied, if I had just told everyone the truth—"

"Stop it," Jack told her. "What's done is done. Now we have to focus on the future and decide what we're going to do."

"Jack," she said, speaking with quiet conviction, "we have to call the police."

"Goddammit, Kat!" He shot to his feet and winced, bringing a hand to the back of his head, as if the sudden movement had jolted his injuries. "We're not calling the cops!"

"We have to," she insisted. "So maybe we can't call it self-defense. But it wasn't premeditated. Charlie came here. We didn't know he was going to do that. And what reason would you have to kill him? So that's...what? Second-degree manslaughter? It happens. Accidents like this." She was babbling, but she couldn't stop herself. "Bars, sports games. Fistfights break out. People get hurt. Sometimes fatally. What's that for a first-time offense? Probation? Six months?"

Jack shook his head. "Then everyone finds out you lied about this place."

She might have laughed at that under different circumstances. "Charlie's *dead*, Jack."

"You'll have to leave your job."

She frowned. "Because I lied?"

"No, because your 'boyfriend' killed someone. It won't matter to anyone you've only known me for a couple of days. They think we're together. That's all that matters. You can't go on working at some place where they think you're a liar and your boyfriend is a murderer. Especially not at a school. Think about what the kids will say."

Katrina was numb. She felt as if her life was falling apart before her eyes. Jack was going to jail, and she was going to lose her job. "I'll move," she said. "Start over again—"

"You just got here. You told me you liked it. You're not packing up and moving because of something stupid I did."

"That's my decision to make."

"You're not listening to me."

"You're not listening to *me*."

"I said no cops," he said firmly.

"There's a dead man in the bushes!"

Jack spent a long moment looking at her, appraising her. Then he said, "There's something I haven't told you. It's about my past. When I told you about my fighting, I didn't tell you everything. Some of the tournaments I competed in were legal, some weren't. Pit fighting stuff. My last fight was, I knocked the guy out, but the thing is, he never got up."

"You killed him?" she said numbly.

"I elbowed him in the eye. The socket shattered..." He shrugged. "The next week the cops busted up the fighting ring. My promoter was arrested and told them everything. I'd already come up the coast to Washington by then. Plan was to go to Canada. I figured it would be best to wait a little before crossing the border..."

"Which is why you're in Leavenworth." She shook her head. She should have known Jack was too good to be true. She wanted to laugh. She wanted to cry.

"You see the problem?" he said. "I tell the cops what happened with Charlie, my name goes in the system, bulletins pop up, and I go to prison for a long time."

"But they were both accidents," she said stubbornly, angrily.

"A judge or jury isn't going to have much sympathy for someone who's killed two men with his bare hands, accident or not."

"So what do you propose we do?" she demanded. "Charlie said he had a wife. She'll know he came here. We can't just leave him in the bushes."

"We make it look like an accident."

"But it *was* an accident."

"I mean a car accident."

Katrina looked at him skeptically.

"We put his body in the pickup," Jack told her. "I'll drive it. You follow in the Porsche. Charlie said he lived in Skykomish. That's west of here. When we get near the town, we make it look like he ran off the road."

"He just drives off?"

"Maybe he falls asleep. Maybe a deer runs in front of him. It doesn't matter. His death won't be suspicious. This will be over."

Katrina was silent, incredulous that she was even considering Jack's plan. Because if she helped him pull it off, she would be an accomplice to murder. But if she didn't, Jack would go to jail, maybe for a long, long time.

"Kat," Jack said softly but resolutely. He sat down beside her and took her hand. "Charlie's dead. There's nothing we can do to change that. But we can change the future. Either we report the death and your life here gets ruined and I go to prison, or we do what I'm suggesting."

"We'll get caught," she said. "Something will go wrong."

"Nothing will go wrong."

"How can you be so sure?"

"You have to trust me."

Suddenly Katrina was consumed by a deterministic feeling she was already on a path she could not change. Because Jack was right. Charlie was dead. There was nothing they could do about that. And she knew she wouldn't be able to live with the knowledge that Jack was rotting away in a tiny cell because of the chain of events that stemmed from a stupid white lie she'd told.

Jack held her eyes. "Kat?"

"Dammit, Jack," she said.

CHAPTER 17

Zach was pressed against the trunk of a tree, still as a tombstone. Blood was thumping in his ears, and his legs felt rubbery like they might give at any moment. Jack had already returned inside the cabin, but Zach was too terrified to move. When he'd shifted his weight earlier, making noise, he'd been convinced Jack was going to come over to investigate. If that had happened, he'd been ready to run and just keep running. Because Jack had not just killed that old man, he'd demolished him—and he would demolish Zach as well if he knew he'd witnessed the entire murder from start to finish. Nevertheless, Zach could no longer remain where he was. He had to check on the old guy. There was no way he could be alive, no way, not after all those bone-breaking kicks that soon became wet, fleshy kicks. But he had to check, just the same.

He looked around the tree trunk, then crept over to the bushes where Jack had dragged the body. He took a few steps into the thicket, pushed aside some shrubs, and flinched, even though he had known what to expect. The old man's face was a scarf of blood. His nose was crushed. It almost looked out of place, as if it had moved a few inches to the left. His mouth was open, revealing a black, toothless hole. Maybe he didn't put in his dentures today, but more than likely his teeth were lying in the dirt over where he'd been beaten silly. Cold moonlight reflected in his upward-gazing eyes, which shone like the ferryman's fare for the trip across the river.

As horrible as his face was, it was his body that caused true horror in Zach, because it wasn't natural. It looked like a doll's body—something stuffed with beans and as supple as a noodle. It was in the shape of a badly drawn S, scrawny arms at its side, knees together. And the chest—that was the worst part. It appeared deflated and empty like an alien in a horror movie had just burst free from it, leaving a womblike cavity behind.

He was dead. No question. "Demolished" was the word Zach had thought of before and the word that came to his mind again. He stumbled away, feeling the first squirming of self-loathing. He'd stood by and watched Jack murder a defenseless old man. He'd remained hidden behind a tree when he could have done something. But what could he have done? It had all happened so fast and unexpectedly. He couldn't have anticipated that first palm strike or whatever the hell it was. Then

Jack was kicking the old guy as soon as he'd landed on his back. By the time Zach had gotten his wits about him, it was over. Five, maybe six seconds. That's all it took.

Zach's first impulse now was to whip out his phone and call the police, or even run down to the dock and tell everyone what Jack had done. But he hesitated. He didn't know all the facts. Didn't know why the old man had attacked Jack, or what was going to happen next. Because maybe Jack was going to turn himself in, and Zach wouldn't have to get involved at all. Or, better yet, maybe Katrina would turn Jack in. She couldn't stand by knowing what had happened—

The cabin door opened and Jack and Katrina appeared. Zach stiffened as if he was going to bolt. But he didn't move. They would see him. He might be thirty yards away, but any movement would draw their eyes. They'd know he had seen the body. Jack would come after him and catch him before he could call the police or reach the others.

So very slowly and quietly he lowered himself to his chest and crawled deeper into the tangle of bushes, moving away from the old man's body. Then he stopped and remained perfectly still. The rich, earthy smell of the soil filled his nose. He scarcely allowed himself to breathe.

"Where?" he heard Katrina say. She sounded shaky.

"Right there." It was Jack. He didn't sound shaky at all.

They pushed into the patch of the bush where Zach was hiding.

Shrubs snapped and rustled. They couldn't have been more than ten feet away.

"Oh, Jesus," Katrina said, barely a whisper.

"Try not to look at it," Jack said. Not "him" anymore, Zach thought. Just an "it"—a clump of meat and bones that if skinned and hacked to pieces wouldn't look out of place in a butcher's window.

"There's so much blood. Why's there so much blood? You said you only hit him once."

"I did. Right in the nose. All the blood's from his nose."

"What's wrong with his body? It looks— floppy."

"That's because he's dead. Muscles loosen."

Loosen my ass, Zach thought. It's because you broke every rib in his chest and probably every bone in his arms as he tried to defend himself.

"Now stand back," Jack said. "I don't want you to get any blood on you."

There was a much louder crackling of vegetation: Jack dragging the body to the pickup truck, which was twenty feet away. Zach pushed himself to his knees so he could see what was happening. Jack lifted the old man into the bed of the pickup. He took something from Katrina—a sheet, Zach realized—and flung it over the corpse.

"I really don't feel comfortable with you driving the truck," Jack said.

"There's nothing to do about it. I can't drive a manual."

He handed her the keys. They chimed as they switched hands. "Stay right behind me until I pull over," he told her. "Then pull over in front of me. And don't touch anything aside from the steering wheel and the ignition key."

Katrina climbed into the truck. Jack got in the Porsche. With a roar and a purr, the two vehicles revved to life. The headlights seared holes through the darkness. Dirt crunched beneath the rubber tires as they swung onto the narrow road. Zach ducked as the two sets of headlights swept past him. Then they were gone, and it was quiet once more.

Zach remained right where he was, flabbergasted.

Katrina was helping the fucking guy!

Zach felt torn. He had no qualms about ratting Jack out. But that meant he'd have to rat Katrina out as well, explain how she'd helped him get rid of the body. Could he do that? Because this wasn't a game anymore. This was as real as it got.

He took out his phone and dialed the police.

CHAPTER 18

Katrina remained a few car lengths behind Jack's Porsche as they made their way west on Highway 2 toward Skykomish. They were passing the stretch of road where she'd picked up Zach, and several taunting questions popped into her head. What if she'd left Seattle Friday afternoon rather than Friday night? What if she'd taken a different route, following I-90 until Highway 97 and going north to Leavenworth from there? Or what if she'd simply never stopped for Zach? All these parallel-world scenarios inevitably led to the same conclusion: she would not have tipped the first domino. She would not have lied to Zach about where she lived. He would not have mentioned the make-believe cabin in front of everybody at Ducks & Drakes. And she would not have rented the cabin to justify what never should have had to be justified in the first place. Consequently, Jack would not have been attacked by Charlie, and he would not have done what he had done.

In the distance the lights of a small town came into view. The taillights of the Porsche flashed red. Katrina slowed also. The highway cut straight through the center of the town. They passed kids on their skateboards loitering out front of a convenience store, a family strolling down the sidewalk, and an old man with a long beard sitting on the bench out front of the post office, not doing much of anything. The normalness of it all made Katrina realize just how nice normal was. In contrast, she was all too aware she was driving a stolen pickup truck with the owner's bloody corpse sprawled out in the flatbed under a sheet. The last time she'd felt this depressed, this lost and confused, had been after the doctors had told her and Shawn that he had an incurable disease. Death, she realized grimly, made you pay attention to living.

They emerged on the other side of the town and sped up once more. Katrina hardened her resolve. She would get through this. Jack was right. They could make Charlie's death look like a car accident. The police would have no reason to suspect foul play. Car accidents happened all the time. She and Jack would wake up tomorrow morning and read about it in the local paper: old man falls asleep behind wheel and dies in fatal crash. The sun would set and rise and life would go on. Come Monday morning she would be back at Cascade High School, going through her daily routine.

It would be over.

But then what would happen between Jack and herself? Jack was a criminal, on the lam, one of society's ghosts. Could she be with someone like that? Never knowing if his past was going to catch up with him. Always wondering if today was going to be the day he wasn't there when she got home.

Katrina shook her head. She was being a hypocrite.

After all, she was now a felon too.

❋ ❋ ❋

Roughly twenty minutes later they were approaching the outskirts of Skykomish. Jack swung to the shoulder and watched as Katrina rolled past him, stopping ten feet or so ahead, as they'd discussed. He hopped out of the Porsche and met her as she got out of the truck. Crickets chirruped from the cheatgrass and coyote willow that lined the road, creating a wall of sound. Other than that, the night was silent. "We have to be quick," he told her, throwing the sheet off Charlie. He lifted the old man out of the flatbed, carried him around to the truck's driver's side door, and shoved him in behind the wheel. He was still flippity-floppity. Rigor, she guessed, wouldn't set in for another hour or two.

"Why are you putting on his seatbelt?" Katrina asked him.

"Because I don't want him to fly through the windshield."

"But that would be good, wouldn't it? It would explain the blood on his face."

"Corpses don't bleed," Jack told her. "He would have a bunch of fresh, bloodless cuts all over his face. The coroner would know he'd been dead before the crash. And dead men don't drive trucks."

"So how do you explain the blood?"

"I know what I'm doing here," he snapped. Then, more softly: "Go wait in the Porsche. I'll be done here in a minute."

She left, looking relieved to be going. Jack reached inside the cab and twisted the key in the ignition. The engine turned over. He went to the side of the road and kicked around in the grass until he found a large stone. He returned to the truck, put the transmission in neutral, and set the stone on the gas pedal. The tachometer needle shot up to 4K RPMs. He shoved the gearstick into drive, jumping clear as the truck lurched forward. The truck roared down the road in a straight line, picking up speed. It angled to the left, crossed the broken yellow line, then reached the far shoulder, where it shot off the road and collided head-on with a black cottonwood tree. The crash sounded oddly quiet.

Jack ran back to the Porsche, got behind the wheel, and drove to the destroyed truck, careful not to spin his tires and leave any kind of skid marks on the macadam.

"Was it supposed to do that?" Katrina asked. "Go to the left?"

"Doesn't matter," he said. "If Charlie had fallen asleep, or swerved to avoid an animal, then he could just as easily have gone either way, left or right." He stopped parallel to the truck. "I have to check it out. Keep an eye out for cars. You see any lights coming, you honk the horn."

Jack waded through the cheatgrass to the truck. One headlight had blown, while the other one shone a beam of light into the forest. The smoking engine was partly obscured by a patch of prickly phlox, but he could see enough of it to know it had taken a good licking. He opened the door and examined the interior of the cab. Charlie's head was slumped limply against his chest. His arms hung at his sides. His wrinkled and bloodied face was turned toward Jack, his mouth open, and he almost appeared to be laughing, as if he'd died while thinking about one last crude joke.

Jack retrieved the rock from the foot well, turned his head away to protect his eyes, then hurled it upward against the windshield, hard, above the steering wheel. The glass spider-webbed around the point of impact. Satisfied, he lobbed the rock away into the trees. Next he wiped down the steering wheel with his shirt, took Charlie's hands, and pressed them on the wheel at the ten and two positions. He believed what he'd told Katrina when he said the police would have no reason to be suspicious of a car accident, but it was better to be safe than sorry.

Lastly he undid Charlie's seatbelt and shoved him forward so his head was up between the top of the dashboard and the windshield. He studied his handiwork. An auspicious feeling he'd overlooked something nagged at him. But on the drive here he'd gone over the plan from every angle, and he knew he'd covered all his bases. Besides, he had to move.

Jack returned to the Porsche, slipped behind the wheel, and pulled a U-turn so they were now traveling back toward the direction of Charlie's cabin and Leavenworth. Beside him Katrina was ashen-faced, her arms folded across her chest. She was looking straight ahead. Eventually she said, "Where do we tell everyone we were?"

Jack shrugged. "Maybe no one will have noticed we were gone."

"By the time we get back it will be almost eleven. The bus will be waiting to leave. Surely people will be wondering where we are."

"I doubt they'll notice my car is gone."

"So?"

"So we tell them we walked up to the point. Let them fill in the rest."

She didn't say anything more.

"What's wrong?" he asked her.

"What do you think, Jack?"

"I mean, right now."

She didn't answer.

"Tell me."

"Nothing."

Jack didn't press her. She'd been through a lot. One hell of a lot. And considering the risk that had been involved—that was still involved, at least until they saw how tomorrow unfolded—she was so far handling herself pretty well.

He shifted into fifth. He was eager to get back to the cabin and tempted to speed. But the last thing he wanted was to be written up for speeding, an indisputable record that he and Katrina had been near the scene of the crime. He kept a steady sixty-five miles an hour.

"It's just another lie," Katrina said quietly as they were passing a rest area.

He glanced at her. "What is?"

"Telling people we were at the point, making out."

"Come on, Kat."

"Don't you see?" she said, and her voice was hard, cold. "It was a stupid white lie that got me into this whole mess in the first place. It led to another lie, and another, and look what's happened."

"It's the last one," he told her confidently.

CHAPTER 19

"Shit!" Jack said, slamming the brakes. The car fishtailed as it skidded to a stop. Katrina, who had been staring out the side window, snapped her head forward, wondering whether in some cruel twist of irony they'd hit an animal, just as Charlie was supposed to have done. But there had been no impact. Nothing lay sprawled on the road in front of them.

"What happened?" she demanded.

Jack didn't reply.

"Jack? What is it? What's wrong?"

"I knew I'd forgotten something."

"Knew what?" she said, working herself into a panic. "What are you talking about?"

"Son of a bitch," he mumbled to himself.

"Jack! You're scaring me. What's wrong?"

He looked at her as if just registering she was sitting beside him. "The blood," he said, shaking his head. "I forgot about the blood."

"What blood?"

"The blood all over Charlie's goddamn face."

"What about it? You said you knew what you were doing." She might not be certain what he was talking about, but she nonetheless felt as though his supposedly unsinkable plan was springing a gaping leak.

He said, "Back at the truck I smashed the windshield, to make it look like Charlie hit his head, causing the blood. It didn't matter if it was dry, because it would be a while before the cops reached there anyway. But I forgot about the other blood."

"What other blood?"

"The blood splatter—the blood that was all over my cardigan. Because if he collided with the windshield, then the blood from his wounds should also be splattered around inside the cab."

Katrina was silent as she let this new revelation sink in. "Is that really a big deal?"

"There's a fucking dead guy back there in that truck, Kat, his face a sheet of blood, which magically didn't get on anything else. Yeah, it's a big deal. A big fucking deal." He paused, then added, "We have to go back."

"Absolutely not, Jack!" she said. "We've been lucky this far. It's not going to last."

"No cars have come toward us yet. Maybe none have come behind us either."

"If we go back, we're going to get caught." She said that as a statement.

"We have to, Kat."

She felt what little there was left of her self-possession slipping, and she thought she knew the hopelessness that someone standing in the path of a tsunami might experience.

"Jack, please—"

"If someone has stopped, then we keep driving. That's it."

"And if no one has stopped, what do we do? We don't exactly have a bucket of blood handy—"

"Burn it."

"The truck?" She shook her head. "I don't know about you, but I've never heard of a car exploding into a ball of flames because of a collision. Maybe in the movies, if one happens to careen off a cliff. But not running into a tree."

"I'm not talking about a big explosion. Just a fire. Leaking fluids, spilled oil, short circuits, faulty carburetors, catalytic converters—these all start engine fires."

"I still haven't heard of cars even catching fire —"

"Because people are usually around to turn off the engine or call for help before a fire gets out of control. But if one started, and no one knows about it, and it's allowed to burn unchecked, there'd be nothing left of the car but a metal skeleton sitting on melted tires."

"And if someone comes by and puts it out?"

"How many people do you know who drive around with fire extinguishers in their cars?"

Apparently the decision was made because Jack

wheeled the Porsche around and sped back the way they'd come. He pushed the speedometer up over ninety miles an hour. It was the first time she felt the sports car break a sweat. The engine whined like a torpedo and the trees outside flashed past in one continuous blur. It was also the first time she'd seen Jack break a sweat. He wasn't sweating, per se. But he was sitting straight, both hands on the wheel, staring straight ahead, intense, a man on a mission.

During the interminable trip back to the scene of the accident, Katrina's mind began exploring what would happen if they were caught. Oddly, it wasn't the jail time she would serve that bothered her the most. It was what everyone she knew would think of her. Friends back in Seattle. Relatives. Crystal. Even the students she used to teach, and the ones she was just getting to know now—kids who looked up to her as a role model.

Eventually, however, Katrina did begin to wonder about jail time. What was the sentence for covering up a murder—or, as the lawyers might put it, conspiracy to obstruct justice? Five years in a state prison? Eight? Ten? She wasn't sure. But any of those sentences seemed like an eternity. And whenever she got out she would have a criminal record. She could never teach again. What would she do with herself—?

Up ahead, Katrina made out a set of headlights. She felt as though she'd been punched in the gut with a steel gauntlet. "Someone's there," she said unnecessarily.

Jack slowed to eighty, then sixty-five, the speed limit. A blue Buick sedan was parked off to the side of the road, beside the crashed pickup truck. A man ran out onto the road, waving his hands. His face was stark white in the headlights. Jack slowed a little more but continued past without stopping. Katrina saw the man's expression switch from distress to disgust.

"He's alone," Jack said. Before Katrina knew what was happening, he'd looped the Porsche around in a tight turn and was heading back.

"What are you doing?" she demanded. "We can't get involved now! We'll have to give a statement. We'll have to explain what we're doing way out here!"

"We're not going to stick around. I'm just going to talk to him."

Katrina didn't like what she heard in his voice. She didn't know what it was, only that it frightened her. "Keep driving past," she said.

The man saw them coming back and was waving them over. Jack pulled up behind the Buick. Katrina was furious he'd ignored her, but there was nothing she could do about it. He was in the driver's seat.

"Stay in the car," Jack told her, then climbed out.

Katrina watched him for a moment, then flung the door open and got out as well.

Jack shot her a glance but didn't say anything. He turned his attention to the man, who was short and potato-thick with a weather-seasoned face framed by a wild mane of red hair and a matching beard.

"What happened here?" Jack asked.

"Damned if I know," the man said, stroking his beard nervously. "I went down there to see the damage, give some help, you know. But, sweet Jesus, I think the poor sucker's dead."

"Did you call the police?"

"Don't got my phone with me. You got one?"

"No."

Katrina knew Jack had his phone in his pocket. Her ominous feeling deepened. "Jack," she said, "come back to the car. We'll go to Skykomish, get help."

Jack ignored her again. "Let's you and me go take another look," he said to the man. "Maybe he isn't as dead as you say."

"I ain't never seen a dead person before—well, no real dead person, you know what I mean? But I'm sure this guy's dead."

"Let's just make sure." Jack put a hand firmly on the shorter man's shoulder and guided him toward the crashed truck.

"Jack!" Katrina shouted.

Both men turned to look at her.

"What are you doing?"

"Go back to the car."

"What are you doing?"

"Go back to the car, Kat."

"We'll go to Skykomish," she said. "Get help

there. Don't do this."

Don't do this? Don't do what? she wondered. Kill him? Was that what she was thinking? That Jack was going to kill the man? She had no idea. She had no idea about anything anymore.

The man with the red hair stiffened. He glanced from Katrina to Jack, then back to Katrina. He looked like a man who had heard something of which he wanted no part. "Maybe I better go for help myself." He turned toward his car, but Jack tugged him back. He lost his balance and fell to the ground. "Hey!" he protested.

"Jack!" Katrina cried, coming forward.

"Get back to the car!" he said.

"Leave him!"

"Go back to the car!"

The man with the red hair was already scrambling to his feet, heading toward the dark pine forest. Jack gave chase.

CHAPTER 20

Bruce Heinrich ran deeper into the forest. His arms were crossed in front of him in the form of a crucifix, to ward off the branches from raking him across the face. He heard the crazy son of a bitch right behind him, coming fast. Bruce's mind was pumping on all cylinders as he tried to figure out what the bloody hell he'd stumbled into the middle of and what he could do to escape. He was no coward. He considered himself strong and in shape, largely due to the last thirty years he'd spent as a contractor in these parts, and ten years in northern Oregon before that, building houses and cottages and such, doing most of the hard manual labor himself. But he was no idiot. The man on his ass cleared six feet and two hundred pounds and looked about as strong as an ox. So no fighting his way out of this. He'd have to hide, lose the bastard in the dark.

A branch found a gap between his arms and clawed his face, drawing a bleeding line beneath his right eye. He stumbled, shouldered a tree trunk, then staggered on. He could hear the man behind him, closer than before.

Who the hell were these people he'd waved over? Fugitives on the run? If so, why would they stop? Why would they want to kill him? The only thing that connected him to them was the dead man in the pickup. But they couldn't have been responsible for that. They'd been driving past.

Unless they'd killed the man? Ran him off the road, then came back for something? Maybe there was a suitcase with a million bucks in the pickup—

Bruce slammed into another tree. A broken branch impaled his hand, below the padded, fleshy lump of the thumb.

"Motherfuck—"

The crazy son of a bitch seized Bruce's shoulder. Bruce let out a startled cry. He flailed an arm wildly to break free and connected with what he thought must be the bastard's face. The man let go. Bruce lumbered forward, cupping his injured hand with his good one. He made it about ten paces before an intense heat exploded in his right ear. He dropped to his knees and brought his good hand up to his ear. Blood was gushing from it, streaming down his cheek, slippery and smooth. He'd ripped it in half. He'd ripped his fucking ear in half.

Something slammed his back. The pain was like a cannonball. He fell to his side and realized he couldn't move—his arms, legs, neck, he couldn't move anything.

Lord, was he paralyzed?

* * *

Jack stared down at the dark, lifeless shape of the man he'd killed. He'd driven his foot into the man's back and heard the spine snap. Then he'd kicked him in the right temple, where a major artery and nerve were located, to make sure the job was done. The smartest thing to do now, he decided, was to leave the body where it was. He knew if he brought it back to the car, and Katrina saw it, she'd never help him dispose of it properly. In fact, he was pretty sure she would go straight to the cops. Besides, nobody was going to find it out here anyway, not in the forest alongside an unremarkable strip of highway. No hiking trails nearby. No Ski-Doo trails. The only thing that would find the man was something with a good nose, a nose for blood, like a bear or coyote. And that was ideal. No medical examiner could comb over a body that was in the belly of a bear. There would be bones left, but that would be all. By next spring they would be buried beneath a new carpet of leaf litter and fresh ground vegetation.

Jack searched the corpse for a wallet and keys, which he found. He made his way back to the highway, pushed past some sagebrush, then was clear of the trees. Katrina was by the Porsche, arms folded across her chest, pacing back and forth. She spotted him and ran over, looking like someone who had just escaped from a loony bin. "What have you done, Jack?" she sobbed, pounding her small fists against his chest. "What in God's name have you done?"

"Get a grip, Kat!" he said. "What's gotten into you? You scared the shit out of that guy with your cryptic talk. You made it sound as if I'd been planning on killing him!"

She continued to pound. "Did you?" she demanded. "Did you kill him? I know you did! Don't lie to me. I know you did."

"Are you serious?" He grabbed her wrists. "You're not making any sense. You're hysterical."

"You killed him!"

"I just had a talk with him."

"Liar!"

"It's true."

"Where is he then? Where is he right now?" He felt her wrists tremble in his grip as if she wanted to yank them free or start hitting him again. He held them firmly.

"He's thinking about the talk I had with him. The talk I had planned from the beginning." He finally let her go and glanced down the highway both ways. "I'll explain everything to you very soon. But not now, not here. We have to get the hell out of here before someone else comes along."

Katrina swayed, as if suddenly dizzy. A hand went to her mouth.

"Don't throw up!" Jack said, knowing a pile of

her puke nearby the burning truck would ruin everything.

He tore off his T-shirt and held it like a horizontal sail in front of her. She vomited into it, retching over and over again. Jack's eyes went back to the highway. No headlights. Not yet. But their luck wasn't going to last forever. He felt as though they were playing Russian roulette, not with bullets but with each second that slipped by.

When Katrina finished puking, he knotted the shirt so it became a small pouch, carried it to the Buick, and tossed it in the backseat.

Katrina was right behind him, a shadow. "What did you say to him?" Her voice was raspy. She still looked as furious and scared as she had before, but now there was something else in her eyes: doubt. She was doubting her previous conviction he'd killed the man.

"I'll explain everything later," he told her. "I promise. But right now we have to finish this. Someone's going to come by any minute."

"I don't care," she said. "I'm done with this."

"Goddammit, Kat! You'll be throwing away your life. Don't you get that?"

Leaving her to dwell on this, Jack ran to the pickup truck. He shoved aside the bush of prickly phlox and yanked up the hood, which had already come unhinged by the collision with the tree trunk. The engine was still running like he'd left it. He unscrewed the oil filter. It was hot and burned his hand. He shook the excess oil onto the scorching manifold and exhaust, then screwed the filter back on, leaving it a little loose so if the fire was investigated it would appear to have been loose before the crash, or to have been a product of the crash—either way explaining the leaking oil and, consequently, the fire.

The oil bubbled, creating a smell of rotten eggs that almost gagged him. Blue smoke billowed into the air in thick, greasy clouds. There was a whoosh as the entire engine burst into flames. Seconds later the blaze leaped higher as other fluids ignited.

Jack returned to where Katrina waited. "You're going to have to drive the Buick," he told her, holding forth the keys while checking the highway once more.

"You said you only talked to that man," she said, confused.

"I did. I talked to him. I threatened him, yeah, but I only talked to him. I took his driver's license and told him if he ever said a word about any of this I was going to come for him and his family." When he saw the look of horror on her face, he added quickly, "It was just a threat, Kat, to keep him quiet." His eyes went to the highway again. "Look, we can discuss the ethics of this later. After you've thought it through rationally, and after you've done that if you still want to give up or turn us in or whatever, then fine, your call. But right now we need to move."

"Where is he?" she said. "Why do we have to

take his car?"

"I wanted him to walk home. Have a good long while to think about what I told him so he doesn't do anything rash. And his car can't be here when the next person drives by."

What seemed like an eternity passed before Katrina held out her hand. Relieved, Jack gave her the Buick's keys.

"Stay close behind me," he said. "I know a place —"

In the distance, coming from the east, a set of headlights appeared.

CHAPTER 21

Jack was already running to the Porsche. "Go! Go!" he shouted at her. "Don't turn on the headlights."

Katrina jumped into the front seat of the Buick. She fumbled with the keychain. There were about ten keys on the damn thing! She jammed the biggest into the ignition. It fit but didn't turn. The next one, however, worked. The engine caught. Jack pulled up beside her and was saying something. She buzzed down the window.

"Don't use your brakes either," he said, then peeled off into the night.

She followed, spending about as much time looking in the rearview mirror as she did straight ahead. The jumping flames of the blazing fire had now consumed the entire pickup truck. The headlights of the fast-approaching vehicle merged into one bright streak of light. She prayed she was far enough ahead to have escaped their reach. Then the inferno disappeared behind trees as the road began to bend slightly. The headlights vanished as well. Apparently whoever was behind her had indeed stopped to investigate the blazing wreck.

The dizzying rush left her, but she still felt as if she was jacked up on speed. For the first time she became aware the car stank like vomit, and she remembered Jack had tossed the puke-filled shirt in the backseat.

Katrina played over everything that had happened again, wondering how it had all gone so wrong. When Jack had emerged from the forest, and she'd been convinced he'd killed the man with the red hair, she'd been numbed, once again unable to think straight or fully accept what was happening. It was as if she was a member of an audience, watching a drama that was her life unfolding. She could see herself pounding Jack's chest, could hear herself accusing him, but didn't seem to be in control. All she could do was watch from that spectator's seat as she refused to go along with what Jack was saying because by denying him she'd thought she could somehow deny that any of this was really happening.

She felt appalled at what she'd become a party to. She knew she should go to the police, tell them what happened, her and Jack's fate be damned. Nevertheless, she couldn't bring herself to do this. She didn't want her face splashed over newspapers with vicious headlines, didn't want to spend years in a cold cement cell. And in the end that's why she took the damn keys to the Buick.

Katrina focused on the road ahead. She could make out the shape of the black Porsche, but only because she knew it was there. When Jack flicked on his headlights, she did the same. A place called '59er Diner rolled past on the left side of the road. It was deserted at this hour. Jack slowed to make the turn onto State Route 207, toward Lake Wenatchee State Park.

Katrina frowned, wondering where he was leading her. She hadn't thought about that yet. She'd assumed he would be going to the red-haired man's home to drop off the Buick. But up 207? Did the man not live in a nearby town, but in the forest? With his family? Unlikely. Was Jack not going to the man's home then? Was he returning to the cabin—with the Buick? That would be crazy. She wished she had brought her phone so she could call him and ask what the hell he was thinking. But her phone was in her handbag, back in the cabin.

They continued north for three miles until they reached Wenatchee River, which they crossed. Jack took the back road toward Charlie's cabin. She could recall the way well, even in the dark. Everything about this evening, every detail, would likely be ingrained in her brain for years to come.

Jack made a right turn down a narrow road with a "Road Closed" sign nailed to a tree. He stopped in a small clearing. She parked next to him and got out. The area offered a clear view of the moon-dappled lake. She figured this was a lot someone had purchased and cleared with plans to build on it.

"I thought you were taking us back to the cabin," she said.

He nodded at the Buick. "Not with that."

"How did you know about this place?"

"I saw it earlier when we came in."

"But why are we here?"

"It's where we're leaving the Buick until tomorrow. I'll come back and drive it to the man's house then."

"He's not going to keep quiet, Jack. He's going to —"

"He won't say a word."

"You don't know—"

"Would you say something about nothing that concerns you if it would put your family at risk?" Jack rested his hands on her shoulders. "Kat, it was just a threat. You know that, I know that. But he doesn't. That's all that matters."

Katrina was about to respond, but she closed her mouth. She'd been through too much. She was overwhelmed. She was angry and mixed up and scared. She simply didn't want to talk anymore.

Then Jack was pulling her close, telling her it was all okay. She resisted his embrace for a moment before giving in, sinking against his chest, and letting the tears come.

CHAPTER 22

It was nearly 11 p.m. when they returned to the cabin. They parked a fair way down the road, so no one would see or hear them pull up, and walked the rest of the way. Jack was once more wearing his white T-shirt. They'd washed the grease and oil from it in the lake where they'd left the Buick, and now it was damp and faintly smelly. He was holding Katrina's hand. The light from the cabin's porch shone through the fence of trees. Something by Queen was playing, and Katrina thought back to when her sister had called on Wednesday to say she wanted to visit. That seemed like a lifetime ago.

Someone cried out, then laughed. More ruckus followed.

Old Charlie would be rolling over in his grave, Katrina thought—if he had one.

They passed the school bus, which was idling, getting ready to leave. The driver, Lance, spotted them and honked the deep horn.

"You're back!" Monica said. She was standing with Graham near the cabin, beneath a blue elderberry, the berries purple and ripened.

Some people inside the cabin stuck their heads out to say hi.

"Sorry to hold everyone up," Jack said. "Guess we lost track of time."

"I'm sure you did," Monica said with an impish smile.

"You know there's a bedroom upstairs," Graham added.

It was as Jack had said, Katrina realized. No one suspected a thing. The knot in her stomach loosened a little.

"Hey, listen," Monica said. "We cleaned up most of the stuff inside already, but you're still going to need to do a proper job in the morning when it's light again, right?"

"I guess," Katrina replied.

"Well, Bob and Steve are still down on the dock fishing. And Graham and I don't want to head back yet. So—would you mind if the four of us stuck around for the night with you and your sister?"

"Where is Crystal?" Katrina said.

"With Zach," Graham said.

"Get out!"

Monica said, "They came by earlier, got some drinks, then disappeared again. No one has seen them since."

"So nobody knows where they are?"

"Do you want to go look for them?" Jack asked

her.

Katrina couldn't believe Crystal had gone off with Zach, especially after she'd warned her to stay away from him. But after all she'd just been through, she couldn't get worked up over it. "No," she said. "Doesn't matter."

"So you don't mind if we stay?" Monica asked.

Katrina would have preferred for everyone to have gotten on the bus right then—herself included—so she could put this ghastly night behind her. But she couldn't do that. Monica was right. She and Jack would have to clean up properly in the morning. So she supposed it wouldn't hurt to have a few others stay as well. It would seem suspicious to say no. Besides, it would also give Jack and herself an alibi for the remainder of the night, if it ever came to them needing such a thing. "Sure," she said.

Monica headed toward the dock, presumably to tell Bob and Steve they didn't have to pack up. Then the teachers who were leaving emerged from the cabin and began saying their goodbyes, telling Katrina they had a great time.

Once the bus was loaded and the bi-fold doors closed, Lance maneuvered the vehicle around, got it facing the right way, then chugged down the dirt road, branches slapping at the high roof.

Monica was coming up from the dock. "Hey! Anyone hungry?" she called. "They've caught like ten fish already—Zach!"

Katrina turned. Zach and Crystal had emerged

from the trees to the east, walking side by side.

"Get some action, Zachy-boy?" Graham said.

"Quiet, Graham," Katrina told him sternly.

"We were just over at the neighbor's dock," Crystal said.

"Sorry about what happened earlier," Jack said to Zach. "No hard feelings?"

Zach looked at him, then looked away.

"Who came by a little while ago?" Crystal asked.

"What?" Katrina said.

"We saw a car drive past." She turned to Zach. "It was a pickup truck, wasn't it?"

"Maybe." He shrugged. "I don't know."

"Sure you do. You followed it."

"No, I didn't. I told you, I went to take a leak."

Crystal looked at Katrina expectantly.

"We didn't see any truck," she said.

"What mushrooms are you eating, dude?" Graham said. "You told me a friend of Jack's stopped by."

Katrina had forgotten Graham had mentioned the truck earlier, while she'd been looking for a shirt for Jack to wear. Her mind reeled for an explanation.

"It was someone I'm doing a project with," Jack said. "I needed to sign some papers. I told him to come by so he could mail them off Monday morning."

"So that was you who left with him," Crystal said. She turned to Zach again. "See, I told you it was his car."

"You left?" Monica said to Jack. "Where did you go?"

"Back to Leavenworth," he said. "We had to get some documents we forgot."

"Did you go too?" Zach asked Katrina.

"Yes," she said, hoping it was the right answer. It probably would have sounded more plausible had she said she'd stayed behind. But she was too worried about saying something that could be contradicted.

"That's a pimp ride you have," Graham told Jack. He searched the parking area. "Where is it?"

"Down the road a little."

"Why—"

"I'm going to get a drink," Katrina said, freaking out that their story was coming apart at the seams.

"I'll join you," Jack said.

They went inside the cabin before anyone could ask any more questions.

In the kitchen, Jack said, "Damn your sister. Our story has gone out the window."

"You said we wouldn't be suspects."

"We won't." He clenched his jaw. "What do you think about Zach?"

"What do you mean?"

"Do you think he saw anything?"

"What makes you think that?"

"Your sister said he followed the truck."

"He said he went to relieve himself."

"And who do you believe?"

Katrina didn't reply. She tried to think of

whether Zach could have followed the truck back to the cottage and watched Jack hit the old man. There was a chance. But it was unlikely. Why would he have cared about a passing vehicle? Especially if he had been off somewhere making out with Crystal? Still, the fact he might have seen something chilled her to the bone. She made a mental note to ask Crystal exactly what had happened when she got her alone tomorrow.

"Also," Jack said, "I was getting a vibe from him."

"What kind of vibe?"

"He wouldn't look me in the eyes."

"You threw him out of the party, Jack. What do you expect? If I were him, I wouldn't feel comfortable around you either."

"Maybe. But I don't trust him."

"That doesn't mean he saw anything."

Jack studied her for a moment, his eyes searching hers. Then, as if to reassure her that everything was still okay, he cupped her face in his hands and kissed her on the lips.

Katrina felt nothing at all.

CHAPTER 23

Just after sunrise, while everyone else was sleeping, Jack drove the Porsche through the early morning fog to the clearing where he and Katrina had abandoned the Buick. The blue sedan was the same as they'd left it, though with the addition of a coat of dew that misted the windshield.

Jack put down all the windows, put the transmission in neutral, and pushed the car onto the slab of rock that led to the lake. Then he gave it a strong shove. It rolled away from him, bouncing down the slope, the undercarriage scraping against the rock, throwing up a sheet of sparks. It splashed into the water, which washed over the hood and flooded the interior. The car floated in one spot for a while, defiant, until the engine dragged the front end down. Finally, the entire thing sank from view.

Jack watched the spot where it had once been until the trapped air had stopped bubbling to the

surface and the water became mirror smooth once
more.

CHAPTER 24

When Katrina woke light was shining through the bedroom loft window. She could hear voices floating up from the lake. For a moment she wondered where she was before the events of the previous night hit her like a slap across the face. Charlie's bloodied corpse. Jack chasing the Good Samaritan. The truck on fire. For a long, dazed moment, Katrina tried to tell herself it was all a bad dream. It wasn't, of course. It was reality, cold and brutal. She groaned in misery. She wanted to curl up into a ball and pretend the last night never happened, but she couldn't do that. She had to face the day and learn whether or not the police suspected foul play in Charlie's death. By the afternoon she would either be in police custody or free. She felt like a gambler who had just placed her entire life savings on one bet.

She climbed out of bed—still fully clothed— and went downstairs. Monica was in the kitchen, boiling water on the stove's old burner.

"Where's Jack?" Katrina asked.

"No idea," Monica said. "I've been up for about an hour and haven't seen him." She cocked an eye. "You don't know? Didn't you two…sleep upstairs?"

The truth was that Katrina had no idea where Jack had slept. After the kiss in the kitchen, she'd told him she needed to lie down. Emotionally drained, she was out in seconds and didn't wake until a few minutes ago. "I guess I drank too much," she told Monica by way of explanation. "Was out like a light. I'm not sure where he slept." She looked around the cabin. "What about Zach and Crystal? Where are they?"

"They took off again last night. I don't know where. I spent most of the night at the dock."

The water came to a boil. Monica made them both mugs of instant coffee. Katrina's mug had the red-and-blue Esso logo on it, below the words "Thankful Tankful '87." She wondered if it had meant anything special to Charlie, whether it had any sentimental value.

Monica withdrew a box of Special K from her backpack, along with a carton of UHT milk. She offered Katrina a bowl, but Katrina declined. She was too upset to stomach anything.

While Monica ate her cereal, they made small talk, mostly about the party—Monica had gone skinny dipping with Graham and Bob—but Katrina wasn't listening. Her mind was a million miles away.

At half past eight, Jack came through the front door, carrying two brown paper bags from McDonald's. Katrina greeted his arrival with conflicting emotions. Relief he was back from wherever he'd been...and mild and uncertain fear. The way he'd acted last night—his calm coolness, his rational persuasion, his apparent lack of remorse at what they'd done—it was not normal.

Nevertheless, her relief and fear were trumped by a burning curiosity. Had he returned the Buick to the Good Samaritan? Had the guy kept his end of the bargain?

She saw the newspaper rolled up beneath Jack's arm and more questions jumped to the forefront of her mind. Had the media reported the car accident? What was the verdict?

"Hope you two haven't eaten," Jack said, as upbeat as usual. He looked around the empty room. "Where are the others?"

"Down at the dock," Monica said. "Apparently morning is the best time to fish."

"Tell them there's food here if they want it." He looked at Katrina. She couldn't read anything in his eyes. "Want to come outside for a minute, Kat? I have something to show you."

It was another beautiful day. The sun was burning brightly in the cobalt-blue sky, lighting the timbered slopes of the Cascade Mountains a brilliant emerald green. Puffy clouds drifted lazily overhead on unseen currents. There were a few canoes out on the lake, as well as a motorboat, sounding like an industrious bee in the otherwise still morning air. Jack stopped when they were some distance from the cabin.

"Did you talk to him?" Katrina asked quickly. "The red-haired man?"

"Drove his Buick back to him this morning. His lips are sealed. You don't have to worry about him." Then he held up the paper that had been beneath his arm. It was the Leavenworth *Echo*. "And nothing in here."

"Is that good?" she asked hopefully.

"Accidents aren't newsworthy."

"But that's just the *Echo*. Isn't there a Skykomish paper?"

"I didn't see one. But I also have the Everett *Herald* and the Wenatchee *World* in my car."

"And nothing?"

"Zip. I went through every page."

"Do you think it just didn't make the morning edition?"

"It's possible. But I doubt it. Whoever we saw behind us last night would have reported the burning truck. If foul play was suspected, editors would have had all night to get the story together."

We got away with it then, Katrina thought, overwhelmed with relief, although the relief was tainted with the guilt of knowing they'd gotten away with something very wrong.

"So what does this mean?" she asked regardless, wanting Jack to confirm what she had just concluded.

"It means," he told her, "that last night never happened."

* * *

Zach was stretched out on the rocky outcrop to the west of Katrina's cabin—or whoever the place belonged to. He'd pressed Crystal about her slipup the night before, but she hadn't given him anything more. She was beside him now, her head on his chest. The morning sun was warm on his face. A breeze came off the water. It should have been a picture-perfect Sunday morning. But it wasn't. How could it be after what he'd seen? He'd witnessed a goddamn murder. A murder he'd never reported. He'd been close. He'd pressed 911 into his phone, but he'd backed out before he'd pressed Send. Why? He'd asked himself that a dozen times since, and he kept coming up with the same answer.

Crystal.

He liked her a lot. It was crazy, but he did. It wasn't because she was Katrina's sister or anything like that. They simply connected. And that was the fucking problem. If he turned Katrina and Jack in, he could kiss whatever he had going with Crystal goodbye. Girls weren't so interested in guys who sent their older sisters to prison. It was a selfish reason to keep quiet, he knew. But the truth was he didn't know that old man who died at all. If he reported the murder, he would be alienating someone he liked—and who liked him back. Besides, it wasn't as if he was going to keep the murder a secret forever. He was just going to be cautious for a bit, see how things played out. What was that old expression? Fools rush in where angels fear to tread? Zach was no angel, but he was no fool either.

"What are you thinking about?" Crystal asked him, pushing herself up on an elbow.

"You," he said.

She smiled. "What about?"

"Just stuff."

"Me too."

"What kind of stuff?"

She shrugged. "You know. Like what's going to happen when I go back to college. Because, you know, you're still going to be here. What are we going to do?"

Zach had no answer to that, and he said, "We should get back to the cabin." He sat up. "Your sister probably wants to leave, and I have to see if I can catch a taxi with someone."

"I'm going to be at Kat's all day. Why don't you come by after you get back?"

"I...um...better not."

Crystal looked at him for a long moment. Zach was thinking about how he could reword his reply, maybe arrange something else to do, just the two of them, when she got to her feet and said, "I think I should go."

"I'll go back with you."

"No, I'm fine."

Zach watched her walk away.

* * *

Katrina glanced over her shoulder at Crystal, who was crammed into the backseat of the Porsche, looking out the window. She'd been unusually quiet all morning. "Anything wrong, Chris?" she asked.

Crystal seemed about to shake her head, but then she said, "You were right about that Zach guy. I should have stayed away from him."

"What did he do?" Katrina demanded. The last thing she needed was for Zach to start screwing up her sister's life as well.

"Nothing." She frowned. "I mean, we got along great and everything, right? Then this morning we went for a walk, hung out by the water. I asked him about, you know, what's going to happen with us later on because I'm at college and everything. And he brushed me off."

"I told you to stay away from—"

"I know what you told me. Okay, Kat? I don't need you to remind me."

"Sorry, Chris. It's just that—forget it."

"He has a few marbles loose," Jack said.

"That's what you say," Crystal said. "I don't think so. He's nice."

"The best thing you can do, Chris," Katrina told her, "is to forget about him. You'll find someone else. By the way, what time is your bus?"

"Whenever," she said. "They leave regularly. Just drop me off at the station. I'll wait around."

"You don't want to stay for dinner? We can make it early."

"It's okay. I have all my stuff I brought with me anyway. I'll come back and visit again. I think I just want to go back to campus now."

"I have a question for you," Jack said, lifting his eyes to the rearview mirror. "It's about last night. When you and Zach met us back at the cabin, just after everyone else had left on the bus, you said something about Zach following my friend's truck. But Zach said he was taking a leak. Which was it?"

"Why?"

"I'm just curious."

"Why?"

"It's complicated, Chris," Katrina said. "Just answer Jack."

She shrugged. "We were sitting down on the neighbor's dock and this truck drove by. I thought Zach said something about seeing who it was. Maybe he didn't though. Maybe he just needed to use the bathroom. We drank a lot. I can't remember."

"Why would he have wanted to see who it was?" Katrina asked.

"I have no idea—" She paused midsentence. "Oh, shoot."

"What?" Katrina turned farther in her seat.

"Umm. I might have let it slip that the cabin wasn't really yours."

"What!" Katrina said. "To Zach? What did you say?"

"I'm not sure. I can't remember everything. I was pretty drunk."

"Tell me, Chris!"

"I don't know! He was talking about the cabin like it was mine. I told him it wasn't. He said yeah, yeah, your sister's place, and I started to say it wasn't yours either."

"So he might have wanted to find out what was going on?" Jack asked.

"Maybe. Who cares? What's the big deal?"

"How long was he gone?" Jack asked.

"Not long, I don't think. Like a couple of minutes, maybe."

Katrina realized this was turning into an interrogation, but she didn't care. The implications of Crystal's revelation were staggering. If Zach had seen Jack murder the old man, well...he was Zach. He wasn't going to keep quiet, not in a million years. He was going to sing like a canary on a world tour, and he was going to do it with a big smile on his face.

Had he already? Would the police be waiting for her back at her house?

Katrina and Jack exchanged glances. She saw concern in his eyes, and that's probably what he saw in hers. She asked, "What did he say when he returned?"

Crystal shook her head. "Nothing. He didn't say anything." Her voice became petulant. "Are you guys going to tell me what the big deal is? You're acting weird, you know that?"

"Someone keyed my friend's truck," Jack told her.

"Oh my God!" Crystal exclaimed.

"All along the driver's door," Jack said. "We don't know who did it."

"Why would Zach do anything like that?"

"He's not exactly my best friend. Not after I showed him the door."

"I don't think he would do that."

"I'm not saying it was Zach. I just want to rule him out."

The car fell silent. Crystal was a dead end; she knew nothing more helpful. To lighten the mood, Katrina changed the topic to what Crystal had planned the following week at school, and they continued on that track until they pulled up to the Kwik Stop on the corner of Highway 2 and Icicle Road at the western edge of Leavenworth.

Crystal went inside the service station to check the Greyhound bus schedule and returned a minute later to inform them a bus would be arriving in forty minutes. Katrina offered to wait with her, but she said she had a book to read and would be fine by herself. So they hugged, said it was good to see each other again, and promised to catch up again soon.

As Jack pulled back onto the highway, Katrina said, "What if Zach already called the police? What if they're at my house, waiting?"

"They won't be."

"How do you know?"

"Because he hasn't told them anything."

"But how can you know?"

"If he had, he would have done it last night. The cops would have come up to Charlie's cabin to investigate. The fact they didn't means he never called them."

"So you think Zach didn't see anything?"

"Maybe," Jack said. "I don't know. But I'm going to find out."

She frowned. "What do you mean? You can't just go up and ask him whether he saw you kill someone."

"That's exactly what I'm going to do." He made a left onto Ski Hill Drive.

"But what if he didn't see anything?"

"What if he did?"

"Then he would have called the police by now, right? Or he would have at least said something to one of us. You saw him last night. He didn't act like he saw something."

"I told you I got a vibe from him."

"And I told you he had good reason to be uncomfortable around you."

"Because I kicked him out of the party? Or because he saw me hit Charlie?"

"No, Jack." She was shaking her head. "I'm going

to see him tomorrow at school. I'll be able to read him. Let me deal with it."

"Fuck that, Kat! He might be considering calling the police right now. I'm not waiting around for a day to see what he decides to do. Now listen." He swung left onto Wheeler Street. "After I drop you off, I'm going to drive over to his place and have a friendly talk with him, to feel things out. I should be able to tell whether he knows anything or not."

Jack pulled up to her long driveway, but Katrina didn't get out of the car. "How are you going to explain an unannounced visit to his house?" she asked. "You don't think that will look suspicious?"

"I'll tell him I want to apologize."

Katrina hesitated, thinking it through. She said, "Fine. But I'm coming too."

"No way," Jack said. "You'll make him nervous."

"*I'll* make him nervous? You're the one he's scared of."

"It will be strange, the two of us going there."

"No stranger than you showing up alone."

"I'm not arguing this, Kat. And we're wasting time."

Katrina shook her head angrily. Trying to change Jack's mind, she was finding out, was about as easy as moving a mountain with a shovel. "Whatever," she snapped. "Do what you want. You'll do it anyway." She was halfway out of the car when she had a terrible thought. "Jack," she said, looking through the open door, "you're only going to talk to him, right?"

"Jesus Christ, Kat. What do you think I'm going to do? Break his knees?"

She didn't know. Break his knees? Or something worse?

"Promise me you're only going to talk to him."

Jack scowled. "I'm not going to lay a hand on his fucking precious body, okay?"

Katrina flinched at the acid in his words.

"Sorry," he said, his tone softening. "But I need to get this sorted out."

"You don't know where he lives."

"I'll find him, don't worry."

Katrina closed the door and stepped to the curb. Jack wheeled the Porsche around in a tight U-turn, then roared off down the street.

CHAPTER 25

Zach was sitting on the sofa in his basement with a hundred things on his mind when there was a knock at the door. He frowned. Nobody ever came by his place. He waited. There was another rat-tat-tat, loud and sharp as if whoever was knocking was wearing a ring, and the ring was doing the knocking. His landlady? But he wasn't behind on any bills.

More knocking, louder.

Zach's frown deepened. Maybe it was those Jehovah's Witnesses who'd come around last week, an old lady and a skinny girl dressed like Punky Brewster. They read him a passage from the Bible and asked him if he believed it. He asked them if they believed in Smurfs, then shut the door in their faces.

Bang, bang, bang.

What the fuck? Zach went up the stairs, wondering if maybe he should ignore the knocking altogether. He pushed aside the curtain that covered the window in the door and was shocked to discover Jack standing on the other side of the glass.

A wild impulse to lock the door and return downstairs swept through him. But he got hold of himself and opened the door. "Yeah?" he said cautiously.

"Hiya, Zach," Jack said. "How you doing, champ?"

"What do you want?"

Jack smiled but his black eyes were unreadable. "I think we need to have ourselves a talk," he said. "Just you and me."

Zach's fear was immediately confirmed. Somehow Jack knew he had seen him murder the old man. In which case opening the door had been a very big mistake.

"It won't take long," Jack added, and stepped inside, forcing Zach to retreat backward. There wasn't much room to maneuver on the small landing, and he stumbled down the stairs, almost falling on his ass.

"Why are you so jumpy, Zach?" Jack said, staring down at him.

"This is trespassing."

Jack closed the door behind him. He turned the deadbolt, which made a solid click as it slid home. He came down the stairs. "Trespassing, huh? I thought you said come in."

Zach backed up across the basement, putting the sofa between himself and Jack. "What do you want?"

"Like I said. Just to talk." He stopped on the other side of the sofa so about three feet were separating the two of them. He nodded to one of the armchairs. "Take a seat, why don't you?"

"I'd prefer not to."

"Sit down, Zach." His voice was steel. Zach sat in the chair farthest from Jack. "That's a good kid. I think you're catching on. When I say something, you listen. Now, we're going to have that talk, you and me, and you're going to answer some questions truthfully. Got that?"

"Yeah."

"What's that?"

"I said, 'yeah.'"

Jack strolled in a circle around the room as if he were taking a leisurely walk in the park. Eventually he stopped in front of a framed photograph of Zach's parents that was sitting on a shelf screwed into the wall. He picked it up and examined it. Zach glanced at the stairs, wondering what his chances were of getting up them and out the door before Jack got him.

Slim, he knew. Especially with the deadbolt in place. Still, he considered trying. Because Jack was a goddamn crazy murderer—a crazy murderer who was now standing in his home, looking at a picture of his parents.

Zach stood up, not to run, but because he was too anxious to sit any longer.

"Sit your ass back down," Jack said.

"Get the hell out of my house," Zach said.

Still holding the picture, Jack came over to Zach, grabbed a fistful of his shirt, and pulled him so close Zach could see a hairline scar on Jack's chin and smell the musky-woody scent of his cologne. "I can break you in half," he said. "Remember that, champ." He shoved Zach backward, so he collapsed into the chair.

Zach said, "A friend of mine is coming by in a couple of minutes."

"I was under the impression you didn't have any friends."

"His name's Rob. He lives down the road."

"You know," Jack said, clearly not buying the bluff, "originally I came by to apologize to you."

"Apology accepted," he said quickly.

"It's not that easy anymore," Jack said.

"Why not?"

"Because the situation has changed."

"How?"

"Actions speak louder than words."

Zach did his best to look clueless.

"Don't bullshit me, Zach."

"I don't know what you're talking about."

"When you opened the door, you were scared. Why's that, Zach? What reason do you have to be scared of me?"

"Because you tried to beat me up last night."

"Good try, Zach, but no. If I had wanted to beat you up last night, you wouldn't be standing today. You wouldn't even be sitting. You'd be lying in a hospital bed begging the doctor for more morphine because you hurt so bad." He glanced at the picture in his hand, hefted it, as if testing the weight of the silver frame, then sat in the armchair opposite Zach. "Let's talk about Katrina's sister Crystal, why don't we? I'm still not clear on what she meant when she said you followed my friend's pickup back to the cabin."

"I was taking a piss," he said.

"That's not what she said."

"She's wrong." He added, "Why would I care about a stupid pickup truck?"

"Let me tell you why," Jack said, leaning forward. "I think you have a grudge against Kat because you're a stupid little shit and she wants nothing to do with you. I think when Crystal let it slip that the cabin wasn't Kat's, you followed the truck to see what you could dig up on her. Are you following me?"

"I don't know what you're talking about."

"Don't dick around with me here, Zach. I *know*. Get that through your fucking thick head. So what we've got to do now is decide what we're going to do about this predicament we're in."

"It's not a predicament," he said. "I'm cool with it."

"How so?"

"I won't tell anyone anything."

"And I'm supposed to trust you?" Jack was speaking conversationally, had been for most of the "talk," and there was something about that which prickled Zach's skin. "You already told me you don't like me," he went on. "I bet the first thing you're going to want to do is tell someone what you know. And then they'll tell someone. You know how it goes."

"I won't tell anyone anything."

"When you're drunk?"

"No, I swear."

"What about the cops?"

"No, never."

"Because if you ever tell anyone," he said, "even hint at it, I will track you down and kill you, do you understand that?"

"Yes."

"Louder."

"Yes!"

"Good." He sat back. "But I'm not satisfied yet."

Zach groaned inwardly.

"You know why I'm not satisfied?" Jack said. "Because you're a sneaky little rat. I can tell that. Everyone can. It's something you have to work on, Zach. I know how little shits like you work. I bet you think you can report me, then go and lay low somewhere until I'm arrested, isn't that right?"

"I wasn't thinking that."

"Sure you were, Zach. Because you're a sneaky little rat." Jack stood suddenly. He still held the picture of Zach's parents in his hand. He focused on it. "Your mother. She's pretty. What does she do?"

"She's a lawyer."

"You don't want to see any harm come to her, do

you?"

Zach didn't say anything.

"Because," Jack added, "if something were to happen to your mother, it would be your fault. You would be responsible. You do know that, don't you, Zach?" He paused to let what he was saying sink in. "I have a friend. I'm going to call him when I leave this dump of yours. I'm going to tell him to kill your mom if I ever go to jail. Run her down while she's crossing the street out in front of her law office maybe. Rape and murder her in a park maybe. Something like that. My friend is creative."

Zach hated Jack for threatening his mom like this; he wanted to tell the fucker to go fuck himself. But that wouldn't help him any, of course. Jack might lose it and punch him the way he'd punched that old man. Then he might rip out the gas line to the stove and shove some newspaper in the toaster. Blow the entire house, and his landlady upstairs, to smithereens. Zach wouldn't put that past Jack. He wouldn't put anything past the lunatic.

"Are we clear?" Jack asked.

Zach nodded.

Without taking his eyes off him, Jack dropped the picture to the floor. Glass shattered. He picked up the frame, shook away the jagged shards, and peeled the photo out.

"I'm going to keep this," he said. "For reference."

He went up the stairs and left.

CHAPTER 26

After Jack sped off to speak with Zach, Katrina went inside the bungalow and made green tea, thinking it would calm her nerves. It didn't, and she tossed it down the sink after two sips. She ended up wandering around the bungalow, finding the unfurnished rooms a reflection of how she felt: barren, lonely, empty, as if her insides had been dug out with a spoon. This was the first time she'd been alone since Jack had told her that Charlie was dead, that he needed her help to make his death look like an accident, and his iron steadfastness and confidence had left a vacuum in his departure, which was filling up with growing despair. What had seemed like a bad idea to begin with now seemed utterly unthinkable. How had she ever gone along with Jack's plan? The dam of lies they'd built was straining under the pressure of the enormity of them all. Each time they repaired a crack, another one opened somewhere else. It didn't take a rocket scientist to know that sooner or later the whole thing was going to collapse.

Then turn yourself in, she told herself. *This has gone far enough.*

She paused before a picture of Shawn on the fireplace mantel. Shawn had been the complete opposite of Jack, average in most ways. Even so, she had loved him. He'd made her feel happy and safe—and wasn't that all that mattered?

During Shawn's annual physical, he told the doctor in passing that he'd been having some memory problems. The doctor referred him to a specialist, who ruled out the more common forms of dementia. He ordered more tests, including a spinal tap, an EEG, and a computerized tomography. Eventually an MRI scan revealed that Shawn was suffering from variant Creutzfeldt-Jakob disease.

Shawn and Katrina's life was flipped upside down. CJD is a rare and fatal brain disorder that affects a sliver of the population. The physicians—and they had gone to see a number—all told them Shawn had roughly six months to live.

Shawn soon began experiencing involuntary muscle jerks and went partially blind. He lost the ability to move and speak before falling into a coma. Katrina didn't want him to spend his final days in a hospital bed, so she converted the first floor of the house they'd recently purchased into a makeshift sickbay, where she served as his full-time nurse.

Eleven days later he died.

Katrina turned away from the picture. She noticed Bandit standing by the stereo, staring at her, as if sensing the string holding her together was getting ready to snap. She decided to take him for a walk, to do something until she heard back from Jack and learned how his talk went with Zach.

"Come on, bud," she said, grabbing the leash from where it hung on the key hook next to the front door. "Let's get some air."

Bandit smothered her with rough licks while she attempted to link the leash to his collar. Once she had it secured, she grabbed a wool jacket from the closet and went outside. Dark storm clouds had drifted in front of the sun while she'd been inside, and the bright afternoon sunlight had turned a gritty gray. The temperature had dropped as well. It felt more like late October than early September.

As Katrina walked Bandit down the street, she thought about fast-approaching Halloween. She decided an appropriate costume for her would be one of those black-and-white-striped prison uniforms—that was, if she wasn't wearing a real orange one by then.

A little way down Wheeler Street she stopped when she spotted Our Lady of the Snows Catholic Church across the road. It was a white building with a portico and a blue roof. Parents and children and older folks were filtering inside.

Katrina stared at the building for a long time. Then she knotted Bandit's leash around a utility pole and crossed the street. She entered the church and took a seat in a pew. The high ceilings dwarfed the congregation. The light filtering through the stained-glass windows was a brilliant red and icy blue. A hushed silence layered everything, what you rarely experienced outside of churches, libraries, and mausoleums.

The opening hymn began. The priest, dressed in a white-and-purple cassock, made his way down the center aisle, followed by his entourage.

"Welcome to Sunday Mass," he began in a loud, clear voice when he reached the altar. "My name is Father O'Donovan, and thank you all for joining us today in our time of worship."

For the next hour Katrina followed the familiar ritual of Mass: standing, sitting, kneeling, praying, singing. She hadn't been to church for years, and all the while she wondered why she'd decided to attend now. Because if her parents' death had made her discard any notion of an omnipotent, beneficial God, Shawn's death had hammered the nails into the coffin of her belief, all but making her an atheist.

"And the Lord be with you," the priest was saying.

"And also with you," the congregation answered in unison.

"May the almighty God bless you. In the name of the Father, the Son, and the Holy Spirit. Our

Mass has ended. Let us go forth in the joy of the Lord."

"Thanks be to God."

The parishioners got to their feet, chatting with one another, the solemn hush now lifted. They emptied through the church's front doors, leaving only the altar boys behind, who were busy with their duties. Katrina didn't leave. She closed her eyes and rested her forehead on the back of the pew in front of her and tried not to think about much of anything.

Someone spoke to her. She sat back, startled. It was the priest.

"I'm sorry, my child," he said. He was standing next to her pew. "I didn't mean to give you a scare."

"I was just thinking...Father."

"About anything in particular?" He was an elderly man with neat brown hair and creased skin. His blue eyes were kind.

"Yes," she said. "I mean, no. I can't talk about it."

"Sometimes it's better to talk if something weighs heavily on your mind."

Katrina shook her head, at the same time thinking it would be a great relief to confide in someone what she'd done—to ask someone, anyone, aside from Jack, what to do.

"Did you enjoy the sermon?" Father O'Donovan asked. "I haven't seen you here before."

"I stopped going to church a while ago."

"Sadly, that's the trend these days. There seem to be three groups. The faithful who come regularly. Those who stop by for special occasions such as Christmas and Easter. And those who come only when they are troubled and in need of guidance." He paused meaningfully. "If you would like to talk or make a confession, you've only to let me know. I'll be here a little longer."

Katrina watched him cross the nave and enter the confessional. After a good minute of internal debate, she joined him.

She took a seat on the wooden bench. A panel in the dividing wall of the booth slid open. All that separated the priest and herself was a thin linen curtain. The air in the enclosed space was laced with the organic scent of burned incense.

"Bless me, Father, for I have sinned," she began, making the sign of the cross.

"How long has it been since your last confession, my child?"

"A long time."

"What are your sins?"

"I told a lie." She paused, swallowed. She was unable to go on.

"Remember you are not telling God anything He does not already know."

"It was a bad lie," she continued. "Well, no, it wasn't. It was a white lie. Nothing big. But it led to some…some terrible consequences." Suddenly she found the words pouring out of her mouth as she recounted everything, from the night she'd picked up Zach on the highway to Jack leaving for Zach's house earlier this morning. She didn't reveal Jack's name, referring to him as her "friend."

Father O'Donovan didn't interrupt her once, and when he finally spoke, his voice was impartial. "This is a very serious matter, my daughter. How well do you know this 'friend' of yours?"

"We just met."

"Could you persuade him to go to the police?"

"No—he's…he wouldn't do it."

"Then would you consider turning him over to the police yourself?"

"I don't know," she said honestly.

"I think it would be an option you would do well to ponder."

"Are you going to tell anyone, Father?"

"The confidentiality of all statements during reconciliation is absolute. That is the Seal of the Confessional."

Katrina couldn't bring herself to look up from her hands, which were clasped tightly together in her lap. "Am I a bad person?"

"God hates the sin, not the sinner. He is not vengeful or spiteful but merciful and forgiving. Even though you have turned away from Him, He has not turned away from you."

"You can forgive me then?"

"No man, regardless of how devout or learned, has the power to forgive sins. That power belongs to God alone. However, He does act through the ministration of men, and through me, your connection to God's grace can be restored."

"What would I have to do?"

"Are you truly sorry for having committed these mortal sins?"

"Yes."

"Would you commit them again?"

"No—no way. Never." And this was the truth. She was never more certain of anything in her life.

"Your penance is a hundred Our Fathers and a hundred Hail Marys. Also, you will commit yourself to a hundred hours of community service wherever you see fit over the next year."

"Is that all?" she asked, believing she deserved much more.

"Accepting the penance is the method by which you can express your true sorrow. Spend that time thinking about how you have sinned, praying for those you have wronged, and asking God for guidance in how to proceed. God the Father of mercies, through the death and resurrection of his Son, has reconciled the world to himself and sent the Holy Spirit among us for the forgiveness of sins. Through the ministry of the Church may God give you pardon and peace. I absolve you from your sins in the name of the Father, the Son, and the Holy Spirit."

"Amen."

"Give thanks to the Lord, for He is good."

"Thank you, Father."

"Go in peace, my daughter, and may God bless you."

* * *

Jack was sitting on the front steps of her porch when Katrina returned. He tossed aside the pinecone he had been fiddling with and stood. "Go for a walk?" he asked, and although he said it pleasantly enough, his eyes narrowed slightly.

"Bandit hasn't been walked since early yesterday morning," she said quickly and dismissively. She wanted to know whether Zach had seen the murder or not. "So? What happened?"

"Do you want the good news or bad news first?"

Katrina's stomach dropped. Bad news? She didn't think she could deal with more bad news. "Bad," she said, regardless.

"Zach knows."

She experienced a hot flash that left her feeling faint and sick.

"But the good news is this," Jack continued. "He won't tell a soul."

"How can you be so sure?"

"You have to trust me."

She folded her arms across her chest. "What did you say, Jack?"

"I made him a deal, okay? Let's leave it at that."

Katrina felt the shadow of déjà vu. "You threatened him? His family?"

"What does it matter?"

"You can't keep threatening people!"

"Do you want to go to prison?"

"Jack…this is…it's too much for me."

"I'm one hundred percent confident he won't

say anything to anyone."

"Just like the man with the red hair?"

"Just like him. Nobody's saying anything."

"Jesus, Jack." She shook her head. "So what do we do now?"

"We relax. Get something to eat. Dinner, maybe?"

"Eat?" she said, surprised. "I couldn't eat a carrot."

"What do you want to do?"

"I think I need to lie down."

"Hey." He tilted her chin upward so they were looking into each other's eyes again. "If you need anything, even just to talk, call me. We're almost through this."

Katrina nodded, went inside, and closed the door. She heard Jack's Porsche drive away.

Five minutes later the police arrived.

CHAPTER 27

Crystal Burton was sitting on a bench out front of the Kwik Stop, staring at page forty-nine of the dog-eared paperback novel she'd been reading for the second time. She blinked, the words on the page coming back into focus. She backtracked a little and discovered she'd barely read two pages over the past thirty minutes. She'd been thinking about Zach, the books and movies they'd talked about, his crazy head transplant/cyborg theory. Kissing him. Doing a lot more than kissing later in the night.

So what the heck had been up with him this morning? Why hadn't he wanted to do anything with her, knowing this would be her last day in Leavenworth? Had last night meant a lot more to her than it had to him? Or had she simply read him wrong? Had his brush-off been less about him not liking her, and more about the fact he was here and she in Seattle?

She should have asked him this. She should

have told him she wasn't clingy. She wasn't going to call or Skype every day. She would have been fine simply hanging out every once in a while. Nothing serious.

The Greyhound bus appeared on Highway 2. It pulled into the vast parking lot and stopped next to the gas pumps. It was hissing and groaning and seemed to sigh with relief as the doors folded open and the passengers disembarked for a smoke or bathroom break. Crystal stood, slung her bag over her shoulder, but she didn't get on the bus.

She went to the payphone outside the service station, relieved to find the white pages in the hard plastic case had not yet been replaced by automated directory assistance. She fingered through the thin book. There were only two listings for "Marshall" in Leavenworth. Halleluiah for small towns. She dug a pen and a scrap of paper out of her bag and scribbled down both addresses. Next, she looked up the number for the taxi service and ordered a cab. One arrived five minutes later, by which time the dark sky had begun to spit rain. She showed the driver both addresses and asked him to take her to whichever was closer.

The first house was on Benton Street across from a Lutheran church. It featured impressive Greek columns and a semicircular fanlight over the front door. Two cast-iron hounds sat on the front porch. Crystal doubted this was Zach's place. Then again, perhaps he lived with his parents.

She climbed the porch, knocked on the door,

and was immediately greeted by barking dogs. A middle-aged woman opened the door, holding a baby. She eyed Crystal through the screen. "Yes?"

"Hi—can I speak to Zach, please?"

The woman frowned. "Can I ask what this is about?"

So it was Zach's parent's house, after all. "I'd just like to speak with him."

The woman cast Crystal a final glance before disappearing inside. A short time later a robust man with a shock of salt-and-pepper hair appeared in the doorway. He looked at Crystal curiously. His wife stood close watch behind.

"Hi," Crystal said. "Can I speak to Zach?"

"Go ahead."

"You're Zach?"

"I believe I am."

"I'm sorry—I have the wrong address."

She returned to the waiting cab and told the driver to take her to the second address on Birch Street. The house needed a coat of paint, the shutters were askew, and the lawn was overgrown.

This was more like it.

She asked the driver to wait again, then knocked on the front door. A ghoulish-looking woman in her seventies answered. "Who are you?" she snapped.

"Umm—may I speak with Zach, please?"

"Side door. Lives in the basement."

Crystal paid the taxi driver, then went to the house's side door. She rubbed the raindrops from her face, pushed her hair back behind her ears, and knocked. There was no answer. She knocked again, louder.

A curtain in the door window moved. Zach peered out. His face disappeared and the door opened. "Hey, Chris," he said, frowning and looking past her. "This is a surprise."

"I took a taxi here," she said, feeling suddenly foolish. He was going to think she was a stalker or something.

"You by yourself?" he asked.

"Me? Yeah. I—well, I just wanted..."

He opened the door farther. "Come in, you're wet."

Crystal followed Zach down the stairs to a wood-paneled basement with oak-colored carpet.

They stood in what she guessed you'd call the living room for a few seconds, awkwardly, before he said, "Want some coffee or tea or something to warm up?"

"Sure," she said. "Tea, please."

The kitchen was small and clean. Zach put on the kettle, retrieved two mugs from the cupboard, and asked her if she wanted milk or sugar.

Back in the living room, they sat on a sofa. "How'd you know where I lived?" Zach asked her.

"There were only two Marshalls in the phonebook—and believe it or not the other guy is named Zach too."

She'd been hoping he would laugh or smile at that, and when he did neither, she said, "Look, if you want me to go..."

"Huh? No. I was wondering because..." He shrugged. "Forget it."

"What?"

"Nothing," he said.

"I thought we had fun last night."

"Yeah, we did. A lot of fun."

"So what's up with you? This morning, now... you're acting..."

"It's not you, okay?"

"Then what is it?"

"Things—they're complicated."

"What's complicated?" she asked. "If I like you, and you like me, what's the big deal? Because I'm in Seattle?"

"I like you, Chris. I do. But there are some things —"

"Is it Kat—that whole stupid feud you guys have? Well, who cares? I don't care what she says."

"Let me get some stuff sorted here—"

A light bulb flicked on. "Do you have a girlfriend?"

"No, it's nothing like that. Honest."

It was a mistake to come, she realized. She stood. "You do what you have to do, Zach. It sounds pretty important. If you're ever in Seattle, look me up."

Crystal started toward the stairs. Zach gripped her wrist. She turned.

"I don't want you leaving like this," he said.

"Like what?" she said. "You're the one with all

the excuses—"

He kissed her on the lips, and then she was kissing him back.

CHAPTER 28

"Yes?" Katrina said, opening the front door a wedge and blocking the space with her leg so Bandit couldn't escape. Her heartbeat had spiked as soon as she'd looked through the beveled glass and saw the cop on the other side.

"Apologize for disturbing you, Ms. Burton, but I need to ask you a few questions." It was the same police officer who'd come by when she'd reported someone looking through her bathroom window. Officer Murray, he'd said his name was. He had his peaked cap tucked under his arm once again.

"Have you found out something about the Peeping Tom?" she asked.

"Afraid not, ma'am. Different matter entirely. Did you rent a cabin from Charles Stanley last night?"

The question cut through Katrina like a knife. "Yes, I did," she said, wondering how much he knew. "Is there a problem?"

"You could say that. Mr. Stanley's dead."

"Oh, gosh," she said.

"Mind if I come in?"

Katrina stepped back to allow Murray to enter. Bandit sniffed his boots. She led the boxer to the bedroom, closed the door, then returned to the living room. She thought about offering Murray coffee but decided not to. She didn't want him hanging around any longer than was necessary.

He pulled out his black notebook, poised his pen above an open page, and asked, "When was the last time you saw Mr. Stanley?"

Katrina's first impulse was to lie and say yesterday morning. But she told herself that was panic taking over. Someone—Charlie's wife, a neighbor—might have known what he'd intended to do. "Last night," she said. "He stopped by the cabin while I was there with some friends."

"At approximately what time?"

"Nine? Nine thirty?"

"And why was that?"

"Apparently we had the music up too loud."

"A long way for someone to travel to tell you to turn down the music."

She shrugged, knowing if she put her foot in her mouth now, Jack wasn't around to pry it out. "My phone was off all night. Maybe he tried to call me."

"Any idea why he cared so much about the music being too loud?"

"He said the neighbors called him. I guess they

complained."

"Couldn't he have asked them to ask you to turn it down?"

"I'm sure he could have."

"But he didn't."

"No, he didn't." Murray was watching her closely. She added, "When we met him yesterday morning to get the key, he told us some story about renting the cabin out to college kids last year. They threw a big party and trashed the place. He might have thought we were having a similar sort of party."

"Seems to me if he had one bad experience with a party, he wouldn't be eager to allow another one to go on there."

"Well, he didn't know we intended to have one."

Murray raised an eyebrow, and Katrina wondered if she'd gone and done it, stuck her foot in her mouth.

"What was the reason you gave him for renting the cabin?" he asked.

"Nothing. He never asked," she lied. In fact, she remembered Jack's exact words: *All we have in mind is a quiet weekend.* "Regardless, it's not like my friends and I are college kids. We're teachers. We're pretty responsible."

"Did the party get out of hand?"

"No."

Those unreadable eyes on her again. "But the music was loud enough to annoy the neighbors?"

"We brought a stereo down to the dock so we

could hear the music there. That was probably the reason for the noise complaint." She straightened, trying to appear both confused and indignant. "May I ask where these questions are leading? What does any of this have to do with Charlie's death?"

"Mr. Stanley was in a car accident last night."

"That's awful," she said, "but I still don't see what this has to do with me."

"Just routine questioning, Ms. Burton. You were the last person to see him alive."

Katrina wanted to believe Murray, but she didn't. "I'm afraid I still don't understand. If he was in an accident, why is there an investigation at all?"

"There's been no determination yet it was an accident," he said meaningfully.

"What else could it have been?"

"I can't say much right now, ma'am. I can only tell you the circumstances of his death remain somewhat suspicious." He licked a finger and flipped a page in his notebook. "If you could just answer a few more questions, I think I'll be done here."

Katrina felt a rush of cautious optimism. Nevertheless, she knew this wouldn't be the end of it. He would come back, question her again. And even if he didn't, there would always be the guilt, the paranoia of discovery.

Then tell the truth now and get it over with.

"Am I under suspicion?" she asked.

"Why would you be?"

"I shouldn't be," she said sharply, more sharply than she'd intended. "But you're making me feel like I am."

"What exactly did Mr. Stanley tell you when he arrived?"

"I already told you. He said the music was too loud."

"Was he upset?"

"He was irritated, I suppose. He was a very vocal man."

"Vocal?"

"He was foul. Swore a lot."

Murray jotted more notes in his notebook. She wished she knew what he was writing. Her eyes flicked to the words on the page, but she couldn't read upside-down. Sensing he was about to look back up, she tugged her eyes away.

Murray said, "So he told you to turn down the music? What happened next?"

"We showed him the place."

"Who is we?"

Dammit, she thought. "Just another person at the party."

"Another teacher?"

"Well, no. He's not a teacher. I'm involved with him."

"What's his name?"

Would they run it? Find out about Jack's past? God, she was ruining everything! Right at the end, she was going to blow it all.

"Ma'am?"

"Jack Reeves," she told him.

"So you and Mr. Reeves showed Mr. Stanley around. And then what?"

"He was satisfied the place was still in good order. We told him we'd turn down the music. That's it, I believe."

"Did anyone at the party other than you and Mr. Reeves say anything to Mr. Stanley? Perhaps something that might have provoked him?"

"No. Only Jack and I spoke to him."

"No one else saw him?"

"No."

"And he left after that. You saw him leave?"

"Yes."

"Did he say where he was going?"

"I imagine he was going home."

"But he didn't tell you?"

"No, I don't believe he did."

"No one followed him?"

She hesitated. Had one of the neighbors seen Jack's Porsche follow the pickup truck? "Not that I'm aware of."

A thoughtful pause, pen poised. "Earlier today I spoke to his neighbors. They told me they saw two vehicles pass by their place last night. Mr. Stanley's cabin is the last one on the point."

"I don't know who it could have been."

"How many vehicles were at the cabin?"

"Only two. Everyone came on a school bus. Jack and I drove."

"In Mr. Reeves's car?"

"Yes."

"Could you tell me the make and model?"

"You know, Officer Murray, I think I've been patient with these questions. But I'm not sure I like the direction you're taking in this conversation. Why would you need to know a description of Jack's car?"

"Process of elimination, ma'am. I assure you, it is nothing more than that."

"It's a Porsche. Black. I wouldn't know the model. I'm not familiar with cars."

Murray wrote that down. "Is it possible, Ms. Burton, that Mr. Reeves may have left without your knowledge?"

Process of elimination, my ass. "To follow Charlie? Why in heaven's name would he do that?" She shook her head. "I'm sorry, but this is absurd. I think I'm done here."

"Did Mr. Stanley and Mr. Reeves argue?"

"Absolutely not."

He nodded. The notebook went back in his belt. "That's all I needed to know. Again, I'm sorry to have bothered you, Ms. Burton. Probably turn out Mr. Stanley fell asleep at the wheel." He made to leave, then hesitated. "By the way," he said. "Mr. Reeves isn't from Leavenworth, is he?"

"How do you know that?"

"I don't recognize the name. I know most people around these parts. Do you know where he might be staying?"

"I don't know. I've only known him a few days."

"Thank you again, Ms. Burton. Have a good day."

He left. Katrina watched as he jogged through the rain to the cruiser. She closed the front door and went immediately to the bathroom, where she thought she might be sick. She wasn't. Still, the strength seemed to have left her body, and she had to hold onto the sink for support. She glanced in the mirror and was relieved to find she appeared calmer than she felt. Then she realized she had to call Jack. Because if Officer Murray discovered where he was staying, she needed to explain everything to Jack first, so they would be on the same page with their stories.

She went to the bedroom, snatched her phone that was next to the futon, and punched in Jack's number. It rang and rang and rang.

CHAPTER 29

Jack was in his room at the Blackbird Lodge dressed in track pants and a tank top, performing his daily martial arts exercises, when he realized someone was knocking at the door. He took the earbuds from his ears and stuck them in the waistband of his pants, next to where the MP3 player was clipped. He went to the door and looked through the peephole. A cop. He frowned but nevertheless opened up.

"Mr. Reeves?" the cop said. He was a decent-sized guy with dark eyes and thin lips.

Jack nodded. "Yes, sir."

"Officer Murray. May I have a minute of your time?"

"Depends on what it's about."

"There's been an accident. I'm doing the legwork."

"Accident? Anyone I know?"

"Charles Stanley?"

"You mean old Charlie? Met him yesterday.

What happened?"

"He was killed in a car accident last night."

"Aw, shit."

"I believe you were at his cabin last night?"

Jack's cell phone rang. He frowned to himself. Not many people had his number, and those who did rarely called him.

Katrina?

He did the math, making connections. The cop must have spoken with her first. That was the only way he could have found out about Jack's involvement last night. And if that was the case, he needed to find out what she'd told him.

"Excuse me," he said. "Be right back."

At the desk he picked up his phone. His invisible frown deepened when he saw seven missed calls on the display.

What the hell had gone wrong?

"Hello?" he said, turning his back to the door and walking to the far corner of the room.

"Jack!" Katrina said. "God, Jack. Where have you been?"

"Exercising."

"A policeman just came by my place about thirty minutes ago," she said, speaking fast. "I think he wants to talk to you. I said you weren't from around here, so he'll probably be checking all the motels and hotels. We have to get our stories straight."

"Yes, that would be good."

"Jack? Is something wrong?"

"No, that's fine."

"What? He's there, isn't he?"

"Yup."

"I told him Charlie came by," she said, lowering her voice. "He knew anyway. I said Charlie came because he wanted us to turn down the music. I didn't say anything about him wanting to shut down the party. I said we showed him the place and he was satisfied. But the cop talked to the neighbors and learned that two cars left. He thinks someone followed Charlie. I told him I didn't know who it was, but then he asked how many cars were there, and I told him only the bus and yours, so he thinks you followed him. I didn't know what else to say. Maybe you can tell him you were just going to the store to get some more liquor or—"

"That's fine. I'll take care of it."

He hung up and returned to Officer Murray, who was waiting at the door—obviously listening to every word of his conversation with Katrina.

"Wife?" Murray asked.

Jack held up his left hand, revealing no ring. "So what do you want to know about Charlie?"

He took a notebook and pen from his duty belt. "I spoke with Katrina Burton earlier. She told me you were with her when she spoke with Mr. Stanley when he came by the cabin last night?"

"I was."

"What did Mr. Stanley say?"

"Said he wanted us to turn down the music. Crazy bastard drives all the way from Skykomish just to tell us to turn down the music."

"He didn't come from Skykomish."

"I thought that's where he said he lived?"

"He does. But last night he was with his wife. She's in Wenatchee Hospital. Mr. Stanley was there with her when his neighbor called and complained about the noise. He told his wife he needed to go to the cabin to shut down a party and he'd be back. Only he never came back. Instead he's found way over by Skykomish, his truck on fire."

Jack's blood boiled. He could never have known. "On fire?"

"He hit a tree. Seems like it caused an oil leak that combusted."

"So how can I help?"

"Did Mr. Stanley mention to you where he was going after he left the cabin?"

"No, I'm pretty sure he didn't."

"Did you go anywhere last night during the party?"

"As a matter of fact I did."

"Can I ask where to?"

"Back here."

The cop showed surprise for the first time. "Here?"

Jack couldn't tell Murray what he'd told everyone else at the party: that a business associate had stopped by. That could be too easily followed up and debunked. "Yeah, here," he repeated.

"Mind if I ask why you'd leave a party to return

to your hotel room?"

"I do mind. But I guess you're just doing your job." He shrugged. "I forgot condoms. Katrina and I —you know."

"I see," Murray said. "What time was this roughly?"

"Right after Charlie left," Jack said, knowing the cop already knew this.

"Did you see which way he went?"

"Charlie? Shit, I can't remember. No, he turned west toward Skykomish, had to have. I don't remember anyone in front of me."

Murray jotted this down, then the pen and notebook went back in his belt.

"Anything else?" Jack asked.

"No, that's all. I appreciate your help in clearing up this matter, Mr. Reeves."

"No problem."

"You take care of yourself. Those are some nasty bruises on your face."

Jack raised a hand to his face self-consciously. His right cheekbone was sore to the touch, and his nose was swollen. Some of Katrina's coworkers had commented on the bruises this morning, but that was the last time he'd paid them any attention. "Yeah," he said. "Walked into a tree last night. Can't see shit down by the lake."

"Afternoon, Mr. Reeves."

"Take it easy," Jack said, shutting the door.

CHAPTER 30

Katrina was trapped in a small dark room, surrounded by wraithlike people who had formed a ring to prevent her from escaping. They tightened the circle and shuffled toward her until she could make out their faces. They were people she knew: school friends, relatives, teachers she'd had in the past, colleagues she'd worked with, even Diane Schnell, the VP. She was the one who began the chant of "Liar!" Everyone was shouting it, looking as though they wanted to stick her head on a pole. She clamped her hands over her ears, squeezed her eyes shut, and sank to her knees. Someone grabbed her. She screamed, but nothing came out of her mouth. Her throat had shrunk to the size of a straw. The hand gripping her hair shook her violently. She tried to smack it away. It wouldn't let go. She began clawing at it. To her horror, the hand was soft and mushy. She pulled away big clumps of wet, rotten flesh.

Shawn, she thought. *It's Shawn, come back from the grave to chastise me too.*

When she finally broke free of the hand's grip and spun around, she didn't find Shawn behind her but Charlie, his hair and eyebrows burned away, his skin red and blistered, missing in places, white maggots crawling over the sinew and coagulated veins.

The crowd piled on her, punching, kicking. All she could see were squirming limbs and grinning faces—

She jumped scenes, the way you do in dreams sometimes. She was in a different room, bound by heavy, rusted chains to a dirty stone-and-mortar wall. Across the room from her was a man, manacles around his wrists, suspending him from the ceiling.

No! she thought, recognizing where she was.

The door creaked open, and the faceless butcher appeared. He was dressed in long black robes and a cowl, a wicked-looking blade in his hand. He began going to work on Shawn, carving, slicing, skinning, snipping. Katrina yelled at him to stop, but he didn't stop, of course. He kept on doing what he was doing. When there was little of Shawn left, he turned around, something he'd never done in these dreams before, and pulled back the hood that had always hidden his identity.

It was Jack.

Katrina woke with a start. Her heart was thumping in her chest, and she was disorientated.

She had laid down when it was still light out, but now her bedroom was dark. Rain was falling outside, striking the window like probing bony fingers. Something was beside her. She almost jerked away from it before she realized it was only Bandit, snoring softly. She heard what sounded like a game show coming from the other room. Had she turned on the TV earlier? No, she had not.

Had Jack? *Was he here?*

That possibility frightened her. Badly. She told herself it was the aftereffects of the dream. But it wasn't. Her fear of Jack was very real.

This seemed incomprehensible, but at the same time indisputable. He wasn't the man she'd thought he had been. They might be co-conspirators in a murder, but while it had been eating her up from the inside, he'd been acting as cool as a cucumber, never once showing remorse at what they'd done. All he'd cared about was getting away—

The police officer!

She'd forgotten about the phone call she'd made to Jack, the fact he'd been speaking to the cop at that very moment.

Katrina pushed herself off the futon and stood. Her chest was tight, her mouth sand-dry. She crossed the bedroom and opened the door. She looked down the hallway and saw Jack's legs, which were crossed at the ankles. He would be sitting in the armchair. She had a wild urge to bolt out the back door. But she couldn't do that. She might not be looking out for Jack anymore, but she was still looking out for herself, still unsure of her next course of action, of whether to come clean or not. Because if Jack was sitting in her living room and not in a police station getting grilled by detectives, he must have thrown the cop off their trail.

This thing might finally be over.

She took a deep breath, pulled herself together, and went to the living room. On the TV a female contestant on Wheel of Fortune was shouting "Come on! Big money!"

Jack turned to face her when she appeared. "Hey!" he said, standing.

"What happened with the policeman?" she asked immediately.

Jack explained.

"So he bought it?" she said.

"Hook, line, and sinker."

"Will he be by to see me again?"

"Can't see why. It's over, Kat."

Katrina had expected to feel ecstatic at this news, but the truth was she didn't feel much of anything. Except for fear—fear of the man standing before her.

Jack ran his hands through her hair and kissed her on the lips. She flinched. He pulled back. His eyes searched hers. "Something wrong?"

"I'm still—you know—all this. It's been a lot."

"It's finished."

"I know," she said.

✳ ✳ ✳

Zach sat up in bed, roused from his semi-doze by an epiphany: *Had Jack threatened Katrina to help him dispose of the old man's body and keep quiet about it, just as he'd threatened Zach to keep quiet about everything earlier?*

Shit! he thought, instantly awake and alert. Why hadn't he thought about this possibility before? Because if it was the case, then he wouldn't be ratting Katrina out if he went to the police. Crystal wouldn't hate him. They could go to the cops together. There was still Jack's threat about the supposed friend who would run down his mother. But he never really believed that anyway, did he? It was a bad guy cliché he'd seen in a dozen movies.

Suddenly buzzing with optimism, Zach slipped out of the bed quietly, so as not to wake Crystal, then gathered his discarded clothes from the floor. The only light in the room came from a rice-paper lantern he'd picked up at a gift shop when he'd been in Wenatchee for the day. He climbed the stairs and left the basement through the side door. It was still raining, the sky low and dark. He pulled the hood of his sweatshirt over his head and went east on Birch Street, past Orchard and Cascade. He turned onto Ski Hill Drive and continued along until he reached Wheeler. The street brought back cringe-worthy memories of the night he'd spied on Katrina through her bathroom window.

What had he been thinking?

When Zach reached Katrina's property a few minutes later, he stopped dead in his tracks. Jack's black Porsche was in the driveway.

Was he wrong about Katrina? Was she actually in league with Jack after all? Were they inside celebrating that they got away with murder?

There was only one way to find out.

Zach dashed down the driveway, then cut across the lawn so he was next to the trunk of the big pine, concealed in the thick shadows the boughs created, where he had a clear view of the front bay window.

He never noticed the man in the parked car across the street.

CHAPTER 31

"There's something we need to discuss, Jack," Katrina said. "It's about us."

Jack punched off the TV. "Shoot."

"If this is finished, as you say, well, we have to decide what we're going to do from here. What are your plans?"

"To be honest, this town is growing on me. I think I could get comfortable here."

Katrina tried not to let her disappointment show. "What are you thinking? A few more days? A week? Months?"

"Hey, if you're worried I'm going to leave you, don't be. I'll stick around however long you want. We'll see how things go from there."

"That's sort of what I'm getting at." She swallowed. "I think the best thing we could do right now would be to lay low." She paused. "Separately."

Jack didn't react, or she didn't think he did at first. But something fleeting and dark flickered in his eyes. "Separately, huh?"

"Jack, I've been through a lot. We both have. But I'm not made like you. I need time to sort things out in my head."

"And if I decide to stay in Leavenworth for a while because I think it's such a nice place and everything?"

"I'm saying you can do or go anywhere you want."

"But if I stayed here, you would, what, ignore me?"

"Of course not," she said, although that was exactly what she would do.

Jack studied her, long and hard. It took all her willpower to hold his stare. "You're stressed," he said finally. "Get some rest. We'll talk about this tomorrow—"

Someone outside shouted.

CHAPTER 32

Zach whirled around and squinted through the rain. He was so surprised to see someone in a yellow windbreaker pointing a pistol at him that he cried out in alarm. His muscles bunched, getting ready to run.

"Police!" the man said. "Put your hands where I can see them."

Zach obeyed, trying to figure out what the hell was happening. The cop grabbed his wrists and shoved them behind his back. He was about to clasp a pair of handcuffs on them when the front door to the bungalow opened and Jack came out, followed by Katrina. Her dog began barking. She shooed it back inside and closed the door.

"What the hell's going on?" Jack demanded, glaring at Zach, then the cop.

"Evening, Mr. Reeves, Ms. Burton," the cop replied. "Looks like I caught your Peeping Tom, Ms. Burton."

Katrina appeared bewildered. "*Zach?*" she said.

"What Peeping Tom?" Jack asked.

The cop shoved Zach up the porch steps and out of the rain and explained what happened last week, and Zach realized Katrina must have called the police after he'd fled.

"You sick little fuck," Jack said. "So what now—back for a second look?"

Zach couldn't believe the irony of the situation. He'd come here to help Katrina. He opened his mouth to say something but closed it again. He was too ashamed.

"How…?" Katrina said, shaking her head. She frowned at the cop. "How did you know he would be back tonight?"

"I didn't."

"Then why are you here?"

"I was keeping an eye on you, Ms. Burton."

Zach perked up.

Jack said, "Because of Charlie's accident?"

"That's correct."

"Jesus fucking Christ," Jack snapped. "He had an accident. Case closed."

"I'm just doing my job, Mr. Reeves."

The first grumblings of thunder rolled across the sky.

"Your job, my ass. You're dicking around playing cops and robbers because you have nothing better to do with your time in this hick town."

"All right, Mr. Reeves," the cop said, his voice hardening. "Let me start with Mr. Stanley driving all the way to his cabin from the hospital in Wenatchee, leaving his sick wife by herself, just to tell you folks to turn down the music."

"I told you—"

"I know what you told me. But if I was angry enough to drive the thirty clicks for something like that, would I just leave the party, as you and Ms. Burton both claim? And even if he did, why was he heading home, instead of back to the hospital? Not to mention those bruises on your face, Mr. Reeves."

Zach was listening to all of this with a swelling of hope. He'd had no idea the police had been on to Jack all along.

"This is absurd," Jack said.

"Maybe you're right," the cop replied. "And if that's the case, then you have nothing to worry about, do you? But I'd like to ask you and Ms. Burton to come down to the station with me—"

"Whoa, wait up a sec," Jack said. He hesitated a moment, during which the only sound was the rapid patter of rain falling on the porch roof. Then he continued, suddenly sounding a lot more reasonable: "We don't need to go anywhere, Murray. Look, I—well, I guess I wasn't completely honest without you earlier. It's a long story. Come inside and I'll explain it the best I can."

CHAPTER 33

"Can I speak with you for a moment, Jack?" Katrina said when they were all inside the living room.

"Not right now," he said. "There are some things I have to say."

Katrina was freaking out. The fact that Officer Murray was putting together all the pieces of their crime was bad enough, but that paled in comparison to the fear she felt at what she thought Jack had planned. She knew his true character now, knew he had murder in him—cold, calculated murder, not accidental murder. And she also knew he'd brought Murray inside to kill him and maybe Zach as well. The question was: what was she going to do about it that wouldn't get herself killed in the process?

"Jack," she tried again, "I really need to talk to you."

Officer Murray was looking at her oddly.

"I said, not now."

"Yes, Jack. Now."

Seeing the steel in her resolve, he shrugged, excused himself, then went to the bedroom. She followed on his heels and closed the door. He whirled on her, his eyes blazing. "What the hell do you think you're doing?"

"What are *you* doing, Jack? You can't talk your way out of this. Not anymore. Do you understand that? We have to turn ourselves in."

He looked appalled. "Are you mad? We're doing no such thing."

"Listen to me, Jack," she said, her face inches from his. "If you touch that police officer, I don't care what you tell me afterward, I will not go along with anything you say. I did it before because Charlie was already dead and nothing could be done for him. But I will not—will not—stand by and let you harm another person. If you do, I'll confess everything." Her hands were trembling so badly that she had to ball them into fists.

"Jesus Christ, Katrina! I'm not a common thug. You think I get off on this? What happened yesterday happened because there were no other alternatives. You know how suspicious this looks, dragging me in here? Give me some credit and let me take care of this for both of us. I have a plan. It will work. No one will get hurt. Okay?"

"No, Jack—"

Jack left, returning to the living room. Cursing silently, Katrina followed.

"Sorry about that," Jack said. "Anybody like a

drink?"

Zach said, "I would."

Jack ignored him. "All right then," he said as he went to the window to look out at the now-slashing rain. When he turned around, he appeared genuinely contrite. "You want to know what happened when Charlie came by? I was telling the truth when I told you he said the music was too loud. I told him I'd turn it down. But you were right, Murray. He had driven a long way and he had come with a purpose. To kick us all out."

"Ms. Burton," Officer Murray said. "Would you have a pen and paper handy? I'd like to get the facts straight."

Katrina went to the kitchen and retrieved a pen and a notebook from the counter. Then, as an afterthought, she scribbled "Be Careful" on the first page of the notebook's yellow paper.

She returned to the living room and handed Murray the stationery. He paused for a beat when he opened the notebook to the first page and read what she'd written.

"So Mr. Stanley told you to leave," he said to Jack as if nothing had changed, though Katrina was sure everything had. "Then what?"

"I said we weren't going anywhere," Jack replied. "We'd paid him for the night and had given him a one-hundred-dollar deposit. I told him the only way we would leave would be if he gave us a full refund, considering we had only been there a couple of hours. We argued for a bit—"

"Did it get physical?" Murray was eyeing the bruises on Jack's face.

"Come on, Murray. He was an old man."

"Was anyone there to witness the dispute?"

"No. It was just Charlie and me. Katrina was inside the cabin. Everyone else was down at the dock. So we argued for a bit, and when I realized we were getting nowhere, I told him he could keep the rent but I wanted the deposit."

"One hundred dollars?"

"That's right. He decided that was reasonable, but he said the money was back at his home in Skykomish, and if I wanted it, I'd have to come and get it."

Katrina was studying Officer Murray, to see if he was buying any of this. Because even though she knew he'd read her message, Jack was putting on an impressive performance.

"So you followed him in your car?" Murray said.

"That's right."

"Why not ride together?"

"He never mentioned his wife, so I never knew he'd be coming back east, to the hospital in Wenatchee. Besides, I didn't really care for the guy much. Anyway, this is where it gets, well, murky, for lack of a better word. We were almost to Skykomish when Charlie's truck crossed the middle line. I figured he must have fallen asleep. I blasted the horn. I'm not sure if it woke him up or not—maybe it did and he just reacted too slowly. Hell, he might have had a heart attack, for all I know. The bottom line is he went off the road, right into a big cottonwood. By the time I got to the truck, smoke was already pouring from the engine. I was about to pull Charlie out, but I realized he was already dead."

"How did you know that?"

"He wasn't wearing his seatbelt and was thrown forward into the windshield. His face was a bloody mess. Of course I also checked his pulse." Jack paused as if contemplating something. "I really can't tell you why I didn't pull him out regardless. It was a gut reaction at the time. I've thought about it a lot since, and I think I knew if I pulled him out and waited around for you guys, the cops, I'd have a lot of questions to answer. On the other hand, if I just left—it sounds bad, I know —but if I just left I wouldn't have to deal with any of that. After all, he was already dead, right?"

"So you left him to burn in his truck?"

"Hell, no! If I knew the truck was going to go up in flames, I would have pulled him out. At the time there was only smoke. I never thought it would become a blaze."

Katrina was speechless. Jack was incredible. Suddenly she found herself regretting tipping off Officer Murray. Had she just screwed everything up?

"I have to tell you, Mr. Reeves," Murray said, "if you had reported the accident in the first place, you would have been in a much better situation than you're in right now."

"Believe me," Jack said, "if I could do it all again differently, I would."

Murray tore a couple of pages from the notebook, tucked them away in his pocket, then handed the notebook and pen back to Katrina. "I appreciate you coming clean with me, Mr. Reeves. But I have to warn you that what you did, even though you confessed, was a criminal act. You're going to have to come into the station tomorrow morning and give a detailed statement. And since the incident happened within the township of Skykomish, it'll be up to the sheriff there to decide how to proceed. He might let you off light, he might not." Murray looked at Katrina. "Ms. Burton, may I have a word with you in private?"

"Of course," she said, wondering how she was going to explain herself.

Murray turned to Zach. "Wait here—"

"He did it," Zach said woodenly, staring at Jack. "He murdered the old man. I saw him."

CHAPTER 34

Zach had been listening to Jack's story with growing incredulity and dread. The motherfucker was going to get away with it! He was going to get away with murder!

He wanted to remain silent, wanted to let this thing play out on its own, but he knew that was no longer an option. If he didn't say something now, he never would. He didn't think he could live with that on his conscience—even if it meant sending Katrina to the slammer as well.

"He did it," Zach said, looking at Jack. "He murdered the old man. I saw him."

The expression on Jack's face went from cool satisfaction to hatred so intense that Zach wanted to run for his life.

But then Jack grinned. "He's crazy," he said, waving his hand dismissively.

"A pickup truck came to the cabin," Zach said. "The old guy you're talking about, he started arguing with Jack. When Jack bent into his Porsche to get something, the guy whacked him on the head with his cane. Then he hit him again. That's how Jack got those marks on his face. The old guy started down to the dock, to tell everyone to leave. But Jack got up, sneaked up behind him, and beat him to death. Then he dragged the body into the bushes and went inside like nothing happened."

"That's complete garbage," Jack said. "I told you what happened, Murray. Why don't you ask Zach what he was doing off in the bushes anyway? Spying again? Who the hell hangs out in the bushes?"

"I wasn't in the bushes," Zach said. "I was on the dock one lot over with Katrina's sister. When I saw the truck go by, I went to see who it was."

"Tell us why you went to the other dock in the first place, why don't you?" Jack said.

Zach shrugged. "The party was lame—"

Jack held up a hand to cut him off. "A couple of things need to be explained here, Murray. First and foremost, Zach has some sick crush on Katrina. When he saw me at the party, and he realized she was with me, he made a drunken scene, something he evidently does often. He was going on about how much he hated me. Everybody there heard him. I had to remove him from the cabin with force, which probably didn't raise his opinion of me any. This absurd accusation is simply his attempt to get back at me. Either that or now that his perverted little secret is out, he's trying to bring someone down with him."

The cop studied Zach. "You have anything you want to say to that?"

"Yeah," Zach said. "Jack's full of shit. He came over to my house today and threatened me. Said he was going to kill my mom if I didn't keep quiet about what I saw."

Zach noticed Katrina's eyes widen, which confirmed she wasn't in total cahoots with Jack. That relieved Zach more than he would have thought.

"Theoretically speaking then," Jack said, "you've just risked your mother's life. You're either one hell of a shallow person, or you haven't thought your story through very well."

"If you go to prison, you can't kill her," he said, willing Jack to slip up and say there was a second man, thus proving he knew of the plan.

But Jack didn't fall for it, and Zach turned to Katrina to back him up. She appeared unable to decide whose side to take.

"Do you have any proof of these allegations?" the cop asked.

"I saw it happen," Zach said.

"Did anyone else see any of this besides yourself?"

"No."

"Did you tell anyone else?"

"No."

"Someone commits murder, but you keep it to yourself?"

"Who was I supposed to tell?"

"The police."

"That's what I'm doing now!"

The cop nodded as if he was embarrassed to have considered Zach's story. "Sorry to have bothered you with all the questions, Mr. Reeves, Ms. Burton."

"Kat?" Zach said desperately.

Katrina was so pale she had turned white. Her eyes were haunted.

The cop noticed as well. "Ms. Burton?" he said, frowning. "Wasn't there something you wanted to tell me earlier?"

"It's true," she said in a voice so soft Zach wasn't sure he'd heard her correctly.

"What's true?"

"Jack. He killed Charlie. And I helped him make it look like an accident."

CHAPTER 35

"She's traumatized," Jack said. "She doesn't know what she's talking about."

"Mr. Reeves," the cop said, his demeanor immediately alert. "I'm going to need you to come with me to the station. Now."

"Get out of here," Jack snarled. "And take that lying piece-of-shit pervert with you."

"Turn around, Mr. Reeves. Put your hands on your head."

Jack stepped forward. Zach and the cop were both tall, both Jack's height, but Zach nonetheless felt as if they were half his size.

"Don't be difficult, Mr. Reeves," the cop said, his hand going to the gun in the holster beneath his open windbreaker.

"I said get the hell out of the house."

"Jack," Katrina said, moving beside him.

He shoved her roughly to one side. She fell to the floor, crying out in surprise. The cop whipped out his pistol and aimed it at Jack.

Everybody froze.

"Turn around," the cop told Jack again.

"You're going to shoot me?" Jack said. "An innocent man?"

"Turn around and put your hands behind your back."

Scowling, Jack did as he was told. The cop snapped one cuff around his left wrist. Before he could lock the second in place, Jack spun about.

The cop fired. The report was as loud as a cannon in the small room. Jack jerked sideways as if hit by a sledgehammer. Somehow he managed to drag the cop down with him, smashing the cop's head into the hardwood floor. He dropped the pistol, which skittered a few feet away.

Zach dove for the weapon. Jack lunged also. They reached it at the same time, both grappling for control. Jack drove a fist into Zach's face. When Zach shook the stars clear, he saw Jack clutching his wounded shoulder, grimacing, but holding the pistol.

Regaining his wits, the cop charged Jack. Jack whirled in time to fire off two quick shots. Both hit the cop square in the chest. He dropped to the floor, motionless.

Katrina screamed.

And at that moment Zach knew he was going to be next. Ducking his head and raising his arms, he leaped through the large bay window. Glass exploded all around him. He hit the ground on all fours. A shard of glass punctured his left hand like a skewer. Nevertheless, he barely felt it. He was so hyped up on fear he felt as though he'd just been given a shot of adrenaline to the heart.

Scrambling along the front of Katrina's house, he didn't think he could make it to the street without Jack catching him or picking him off with the pistol, so he rounded the corner and raced along the side of the bungalow, toward the forest that bordered the back of the property.

CHAPTER 36

"You bastard!" Katrina shouted. "You killed him!"

Jack was leaning out of the broken window that Zach had jumped through. Bandit had escaped from the bedroom and was running in circles, barking crazily, likely confused as to who was the good guy or bad guy.

"I had to," Jack said, not looking at her. "He was attacking me."

"You shot him! You killed him!"

Jack faced her. His shoulder was a big red mess. The gunshot had torn a wad of shirt and flesh free. The blood from the wound had soaked his white button-down a bright crimson. Even so, he seemed to be doing a superhuman job of ignoring the pain. He went to the dead cop, searched his pockets, and found a second magazine for the pistol. He started toward the back door.

Knowing Jack was going after Zach to kill him too, she grabbed his arm, twisting him around, and hit him as hard as she could in his injured shoulder.

He roared with pain and shoved her aside. She flew through the air and landed a few feet away, the wind knocked out of her lungs. Bandit immediately took up position in front of her, growling fiercely, his body so stiff it trembled.

"Do not kill Zach, Jack," she said quietly but with deadly intensity. "If you do, I swear to God I will make sure you spend the rest of your life behind bars."

"Stay here," he told her. "It's still okay. We're still okay."

He opened the back door and charged into the night.

Wheezing, Katrina climbed to her feet and followed.

CHAPTER 37

Zach risked a glance behind him and wished he hadn't. Even in the near dark, he saw Jack coming after him, closer than he would have thought given his head start. He reached the edge of the forest but didn't slow. He hurdled over fallen trees and wet shrubs and was soon swallowed by the vegetation, which was good. If he couldn't see where he was going, Jack couldn't either. He only wished he could silence the noise he was making. With each step he was raising an alarm of snapping twigs and flapping branches, all of which were dead giveaways to his position.

Distinct from the racket he was making, he could hear Jack behind him, hopefully having an equally difficult time navigating the thicket blindly. In the distance Katrina was yelling for Jack to stop, to come back. Her dog was barking loudly.

Zach caught his foot on a root and slammed into the muddy ground. Dazed, he lay where he had fallen. He listened. Aside from his labored breathing and trip-hammering heart, which seemed to be beating directly behind his ears, there was no sound of pursuit, nothing but crickets and the hard drone of rain.

Which was wrong. Where was Jack? What was he doing? Waiting somewhere in the dark, motionless, a predator listening for its prey to give itself away?

Zach didn't move. The seconds ticked by. Five. Ten. Fifteen.

Katrina called out. More barking.

Twenty seconds. Twenty-five.

The waiting became unbearable, especially since Zach was becoming more and more convinced Jack knew exactly where he was and would pounce at any moment.

A crackling noise, like a stick breaking under a foot, fifteen feet to his right.

"Zach?" Jack said softly. "I know you're listening."

Crickets. Rain.

"Why didn't you just keep your stupid mouth shut?" A few more steps, parallel to his hiding spot.

"You fucked me up, Zach."

To Zach's horror, he realized Jack had turned in his direction and was coming directly toward him.

Katrina called out again.

"You ruined what I had with her. And I'm going to make you pay for that."

Twigs snapping.

"I'm going to find you," Jack went on in his

homicidal growl. "Then I'm going to kill you. I swear to you, I'm going to rip your balls off and shove them down your throat."

Less than ten feet.

Zach knew he had to do something. But fleeing was no longer an option. Jack was too close. Fighting wasn't an option either. Even shot, Jack would destroy him.

As silently as he could, Zach maneuvered his good hand into his back pocket and withdrew his wallet. He rolled onto his side, praying nothing cracked beneath his weight and revealed his presence. Nothing did. He lobbed the wallet into the trees.

It made the thinnest of sounds as it whistled through the vegetation—but it was enough to send Jack steamrolling in that direction.

Zach used the barrage of noise as cover. He pushed himself to his knees and felt about on the ground for something else to throw. A branch? Too long. Something flat and rough? Bark? It would have to do.

Off to his right there was a commotion of thrashing sounds, likely Jack kicking aside undergrowth, searching for Zach. Zach gripped the bark like a Frisbee and sent it off with a good flick of his wrist. It sounded as if it had gone much farther than his wallet. It made more noise as well. But Zach didn't hear Jack take off after it. The night had once again become as still as it was black. That lasted only a moment before he heard Jack prowling stealthily through the trees and bushes, coming back in Zach's direction.

It didn't work!

Zach began to despair. He was trapped. He was going to die. No, first he was going to get his balls ripped off and shoved down his throat.

Zach groped blindly until he was touching a tree next to him. He got to his feet and pressed himself against it, keeping the trunk between himself and Jack. The bark was rough against his cheek, which was still sore from when he'd gone down straight on his face. The scent of sap and pine needles filled his nostrils.

Jack stopped on the other side of the tree.

They were only a few feet apart. Zach held his breath. Balled his hands into fists. A fire consumed his injured hand as the glass skewer jigged deeper into the wound—

He had an idea.

Wincing, he pinched the glass between his fingers and pulled. It wouldn't budge. He clenched his teeth tight against the pain and continued wiggling the glass in a sawing motion until slowly, excruciatingly, it loosened.

Dizziness assaulted him. For a moment he thought he might faint. But it passed and he held the makeshift three-inch dagger in his good hand. It didn't feel as reassuring as he would have liked.

"I know you're nearby, Zach," Jack said, his disembodied voice close. "I can smell your fear."

Zach was alarmed to discover he could smell

Jack too, the same musky cologne he'd been wearing when he came to Zach's house to threaten him and steal a photo of his mother.

Jack moved. Undergrowth whished. He appeared suddenly, an arm's length away, a dark wraith against an even darker background.

If he glanced to his left, he'd spot Zach.

He didn't. He took several steps forward, and then he was past, his broad back exposed. Zach rammed the shard of glass down between Jack's shoulder blades with all the strength he could muster.

Jack bellowed in pain and surprise. So did Zach as the glass weapon sliced a fresh wound in his hand.

Zach stumbled backward, one lame hand clutching the other, which was already gushing blood. He turned and ran, heedless of what might lay in front of him.

A gunshot resounded. Missed. Another shot. Another miss.

Then Jack was giving chase once more.

CHAPTER 38

J ack reached over his shoulder to disengage the dagger sticking out of his back. But where there should have been a handle were only razor-sharp edges, causing him to slice his hand open. Swearing, he left the dagger or whatever it was in place and spun in the direction Zach was now fleeing. He aimed the cop's SIG and squeezed off two quick rounds. In the aftermath, when the reports of the shots stopped echoing in his ears, he was furious to hear Zach still moving through the forest, farther away.

Jack made chase. With each step, however, he could feel his strength leaving him. The wound in his back was a mere annoyance in comparison to the ferocious, thumping hole in his shoulder, which continued to bleed profusely.

Invisible branches slapped his face and ripped his skin. He charged ahead, never slowing until he smashed into a tree trunk with his bad shoulder. The trumpeting pain, combined with the darkness, distorted his perception so he no longer knew which way he'd been running.

Suddenly he heard splashing. Someone crashing through the water. Jack forced his legs to carry him in the direction of that sound.

A few short steps later he burst through the trees into an open glade that housed a large pond churning with the rapid-fire rain. A crack of lightning flared overhead. Jack could see Zach forty feet out, swimming toward the far shore. He planted his feet, aimed, fired. Zach cried out.

Jack ran a few feet into the water and fired again. Click. He ejected the empty magazine, seated the spare one he'd taken from the cop with the heel of his palm. He rolled his hand over the top of the slide, pulling it back toward his chest, and returned his attention to the pond.

Zach was no longer in sight. He'd disappeared below the surface.

Jack remained where he was and waited. When the weasely fuck resurfaced, dead or alive, he'd put a hole in his head.

CHAPTER 39

Katrina was beginning to lose hope she would catch up to Jack and Zach. She couldn't hear them anymore. It was as if they'd both vanished—or died. Still, she pressed forward, putting one foot in front of the other. To turn back would be to give up. And she would not do that, no matter if it meant she had to search all night and morning.

Bandit barked and looked back at her, urging her on. Apparently he still had their scent.

A thousand thoughts were swarming through her head. First and foremost were those of Zach. She couldn't let Jack get him, couldn't let Jack murder him.

She would kill Jack to prevent that—

A gunshot, surprisingly close. She reflexively ducked her head. A burst of sound from somewhere ahead of her. Bandit took off in that direction.

She charged after him, praying she wasn't too

late.

CHAPTER 40

The shot whistled past Zach's head, splashing into the water ahead of him. Knowing that the next, or the one after that, was going to connect with the back of his skull, blowing his brains all over the water, he took a deep breath and dived.

Suspended in blackness, he aligned himself so his belly was parallel to the bottom of the pond and swam in what he hoped was the direction opposite Jack. He was already out of breath from the run through the forest, and his lungs burned. He knew he would have to go up for air soon. He also knew if he did so, and he wasn't far enough away from Jack, he would be an easy target.

He kicked and kicked harder. Maybe it was desperation, maybe mind over matter, but somehow he managed to get a second wind and kept going for another twenty feet or so before his lungs felt ready to explode once more. Abruptly he touched slimy weeds, which became denser and denser, brushing his face, entangling his limbs. This encouraged him. It meant he had gone the right way. There had been no weeds where he'd entered the pond.

He stuck his head above the surface of the water and took a huge breath. The air was like poison to his overworked lungs, causing him to heave and cough. Thunder resounded overhead at the same time, swallowing the noise he made. He turned in a circle, relieved to find he was concealed by a nest of weeds and lily pads. He made out a lone shape on the edge of the far bank, which had to be Jack.

Zach knew he couldn't remain where he was, treading water. Jack would start scouting the perimeter of the pond soon. Nor could he swim anywhere, no matter how quietly. Once he left the cover of the weeds, Jack would spot him. His only option was to crawl up the shore and make a break for the forest again.

He paddled through the water until he felt the muddy bottom beneath his feet, then he slithered out on all fours like a lizard. Dirt and slime were surely infecting the cut on his hand, but he couldn't think about that.

The blast of a gunshot sent him flat to his stomach.

CHAPTER 41

Katrina stumbled into a clearing. Although there was no longer a canopy of branches overhead, the storm clouds had rubbed out the stars, leaving the night smudged in blacks and grays. The rain was falling harder than ever, pelting her exposed skin and face, blurring her vision. She held a hand to her eyes and scanned the tall grass, the large pond, the perimeter of crowding trees. She didn't see Jack or Zach anywhere.

A gunshot made her jump. She cried out, covering her head and dropping to her knees. Another gunshot. She heard the bullet ricochet off the tree to her right.

"Jack, stop!" she shouted. "It's me!" She raised her head and saw a shadowy figure circling the pond toward her.

"Kat?" Jack said when he had closed to within ten yards of her. He was hunched over, almost lurching. The closer he came, the louder Bandit growled.

"Shhh, boy," she said. "Stay."

Jack stopped before her. His shoulder injury looked bad, but it was his face that shocked her. Lines etched the skin around his eyes, brow, and mouth, making him appear twenty years older. Even in the poor light, she could see he was as pale as a ghost.

Lightning flashed, slicing angular wounds in the sky.

"Jesus, Jack, you need help," she said, hoping to get him to focus on his health, thereby giving Zach more time to get good and far away. "I have a first-aid kit at the house—"

"He's around here somewhere. You go left around the pond, I'll go right. Yell if you—"

"No, Jack. This is over."

"You're giving up?"

"I'm not giving up. I don't want to get away with what we've done anymore."

"Bullshit."

"I wouldn't be able to live a day in peace."

"You'd get over it."

"People are dead because of us, Jack!"

"You'd still have to live with your conscience in prison."

"And so be it."

The look on his face became one of disgust. Then he raised the gun.

She stiffened. "What are you doing, Jack?"

"You think I'm going to let you just walk away

from me?"

That's exactly what she'd thought. It was over. Zach had escaped. Jack had lost. Soon the police would be converging on her house. Jack, who urgently needed medical attention, would be taken to a hospital and arrested for murder. There was no way he could talk his way out of it this time.

"There's nothing to gain from shooting me," she said.

"If you're not with me," he said, "you're against me."

"Jack—"

He aimed the gun at her forehead.

CHAPTER 42

When Zach realized that Jack wasn't shooting at him, he scrambled toward the forest. Bits and pieces of Jack's and Katrina's conversation floated to him. He could only make out a few words above the rain, but from the forceful tone, he knew they were arguing.

Zach reached the tree line, home free. All he had to do was keep going, find his way to a road or a cottage, and get to a police station.

He looked back toward Katrina and Jack, who were little more than dark shapes in the night.

They were definitely arguing. Katrina even sounded panicked. What was Jack saying to her? No—what was he going to *do* to her? After all, she'd betrayed him to the dead cop.

"Shit," Zach mumbled. "Shit, shit, shit." But he was already creeping silently toward Jack and Katrina. When he spotted a large stick, he picked it up and carried it like a baseball bat.

Then he was close enough to see them more

clearly. Jack's back was to him.

Zach gripped the stick more tightly and closed the remaining distance between them with long, careful steps.

"Jack—" Katrina said, and there was terror in her voice.

Jack raised the gun. He was going to shoot her.

Zach abandoned stealth and made a final dash. Jack spun around too late. Zach cracked the stick across the side of his face. Something that could only be blood splattered everywhere. Jack collapsed to the ground with a grunt. Zach was still pumped up on fear and adrenaline and craziness and he kept swinging the stick, bashing Jack's head in as hard as he could, over and over. Then Katrina was beside him, shouting something, pulling him away.

Panting, he stepped back. He blinked and looked at Katrina.

"You okay?" he asked, and his voice seemed like a stranger's voice.

She hugged him fiercely. "He was going to kill me," she blurted, the words muffled by his sweater.

Zach looked over her head at Jack. Katrina's dog was sniffing his limp body.

She looked too. "Is he dead?"

"I don't know." He stepped apart and felt for a pulse. "He's alive."

"What should we do?"

"Leave him," Zach said.

"But he's alive."

"Fuck him! He was just about to shoot you!" Then: "Should I...you know...finish it?"

"Kill him?" She sounded appalled.

"If he comes around, he's going to come after us again."

"Then let's go," she said decisively. "We have to get back to my place, call the police, get them out here."

"I don't like leaving him."

"There's no other option." She retrieved the pistol from where Jack had dropped it in the mud. "And we'll have this."

CHAPTER 43

Katrina's living room resembled the scene of a drug bust gone wrong. Officer Murray's body was sprawled dead center. An arm was bent awkwardly behind his back. Glassy eyes stared at the ceiling. His yellow windbreaker and Polo shirt were blotted red, with more syrupy blood pooled around him. Most of the glass in the front bay window was on the lawn. What remained in the frame resembled jagged teeth. A stack of boxes had been knocked over, spilling the few things she'd left in them across the floor.

"Lock the doors and windows," Katrina told Zach. "I'll be right back."

Accompanied by Bandit, she went to the bedroom, peeled the sheet off the futon, and returned to the living room, where she used it to carefully cover the police officer's body. She found her cell phone and called the police. She spoke to the dispatcher for a few minutes, explaining what had happened, answering some questions, then hung up.

Zach had returned from his task of securing the house. He said, "What do you want me to tell them? The cops? I'll tell them whatever you want me to."

"I want you to tell the truth, Zach."

"But you don't have to be involved. I'll say I saw Jack kill the old man, then drive the body away by himself."

"The truth," she repeated. "That's it."

"Are you sure?"

"I've never been more sure of anything in my life."

There was only one chair, so they both settled down on the floor to wait for the police to arrive. Katrina wondered what was going to happen to her. She could not, as Zach had suggested, dump all the blame on Jack. Even if that worked, she would not be able to live with herself. She'd made a mistake, one with unthinkable consequences, and she had to pay for that, even if it meant life as she knew it was over.

"Did you hear that?" Zach whispered suddenly.

Katrina was immediately alert. "What?"

"The back door. It sounded like someone was trying to get in."

"Are you sure?" All she could hear was the drone of rain on the roof.

"I...I don't know. I think so."

Katrina got to her feet. "You locked everything,

right?"

"Except that." He nodded at the front window.

"It's at least five feet off the ground. Jack would have to hoist himself up and through it. No way. Not with his shoulder and all that glass."

"He's pretty strong," Zach said doubtfully.

"It doesn't matter. The police will be here any minute. We just need to stay put."

"Can you use that?" Zach asked, indicating the gun.

She nodded. "If I have to."

CHAPTER 44

Jack stared at the back door to the house, wondering what to do. The bitch had locked it. No matter. He would find a way in. He had to find a way in. Because that little shit Zach was with her.

The prick had surprised him, just as old Charlie had. But it didn't matter. It had worked to Jack's advantage. Now he knew where Zach was. If he acted quickly enough, he could still have everything turn out his way.

No witnesses.

Jack would have kicked down the door, but he wasn't sure he had the strength. Aside from the fact his head felt like a piñata, the entire left side of his body was numb, the right side not much better. Besides, he assumed Katrina had the SIG since he hadn't been able to find it when he came around.

He stumbled along the side of the house, trying the windows, finding them all locked. A wave of dizziness washed through him.

He crouched and pried the screen off a basement window. The window slid open without protest. His shoulder screamed in protest as he contorted his body to fit through the small space.

Then his feet touched the floor and he was inside.

CHAPTER 45

"Maybe it was nothing after all," Zach said. He was pacing back and forth.

"But maybe it was," Katrina told him over her shoulder. She was peering out the bay window. "Where are the damn police?"

"You don't have another gun around somewhere, do you?"

She turned. "I have a knife."

"Yeah, anything."

Katrina started down the hallway to the kitchen. Just as she was passing the basement door, it exploded open. One of Jack's massive arms wrapped around her, tugging her against him. His other hand smothered the gun, aiming it upward, toward the ceiling. She yelled in surprise, kicking and struggling, but she couldn't free herself from his viselike hold. He shoved her forward, back to the living room. They crashed through the door. Zach, who had obviously heard her yell, had backed up to the bay window like maybe he was thinking about jumping through it again. Bandit leaped at Jack. Jack swung his foot, catching the dog under the jaw. Bandit dropped to the floor, motionless.

"So you wanted to leave me for dead, huh?" he hissed into her ear. It sounded as if his throat was full of razor blades.

"We could have killed you," she said.

"Should I thank you for that?" He directed her arm so she was now pointing the gun at Zach. "Should I thank this cowardly piece of shit for hitting me when I wasn't looking?"

"Zach, jump!" she shouted.

"If you move a muscle," Jack told him, "I'll snap her neck."

Zach glanced at the window but didn't move.

"What do you want?" she said.

"To leave a lot of bodies and let the cops sort it out," he said. "Only now you're going to be one of them, and I'm going to be long gone."

"They'll figure it out."

"I'll take my chances. Put your finger on the trigger."

In the distance came the howl of approaching sirens.

Cursing, Jack adjusted his hand so it cupped hers, his trigger finger on top of hers. "Say goodnight, Zach."

Katrina cocked her arm back, trying to aim the gun at Jack's face, and squeezed the trigger. The slug plowed into the ceiling. But the noise of the blast an inch from Jack's ear blew his head back, causing him to loosen his grip on her.

She dropped to the floor, unable to hear anything except a maddening ringing.

CHAPTER 46

Zach rushed forward, bowling into Jack, knocking him backward. For a moment they struggled like drunken dancers, each trying to keep to their feet. Zach was out of control, throwing wild haymakers, trying to hit Jack's bad shoulder. Then Jack struck Zach in the gut, then the underside of his jaw. Zach's legs turned to rubber. He would have collapsed, but Jack gripped him by the hair and yanked him back up so he had him tight against his body.

The world was swimming. Through bleary eyes, he saw Katrina scuttling away, the pistol aimed at them. He suddenly understood that Jack was using him as a human shield.

Outside cars screeched to a halt. Red-and-blue lights flashed through the window, momentarily eclipsed by a shock of sky-wide lightning. The sirens went silent. A burst of thunder shook the house.

"It's too late," Katrina said. "Let him go, Jack."

"Looks like we're all dying here tonight then."

Zach felt Jack's arm tighten over his throat.

"Wait!" Katrina raised the pistol in a non-threatening manner. "I'll give you this if you let him go."

"He'll shoot you!" Zach said.

Jack gave his hair a snappy tug. "Okay," he said. "Set the gun down."

She did.

"Now kick it toward me."

"Let him go."

"The gun first."

She hesitated but kicked the weapon forward. Jack shoved Zach aside and snatched up the pistol. Armed, he started toward the hallway, apparently believing he still had time to escape out the back, when someone on a bullhorn outside said: "How the hell are ya, Jack? It's been a long time. But what d'ya say? Have a few minutes to chat with your old buddy from Virginia?"

CHAPTER 47

Katrina watched Jack freeze mid-step. He turned around. His face was impassive, but she thought she saw something in his eyes she'd never seen before: fear. He went to the front of the room and flicked off the lights. He pressed his back against the wall, next to the shattered window Zach had jumped through. He shouted above the storm, "That you, Russ?"

"Glad you haven't forgotten the voice of an old friend."

"You're no friend of mine. Not anymore."

"Ah, Jack. But you're too hard on me. I'm not the one who's a wanted fugitive. That's you."

"What are you doing here, Russ?"

"What do you think?"

"How did you find me?"

"News travels fast these days, Jack. When we got word of some Jack Reeves involved in a possible homicide up here in the beautiful state of Washington, we called the locals for a description.

I was here inside of a couple of hours on one of the Agency's planes."

Katrina's mind was spinning. Agency? As in the Central Intelligence Agency? What was going on? Why would the CIA be after Jack? Surely not for accidentally killing someone in an underground fighting match?

Jack said, "You know you'll never bring me in alive."

"Then I'll bring you in dead."

"I have hostages."

At this Katrina stiffened. The whites of Zach's eyes grew wider. She glanced around the room. Their only chance of escape would be down the hallway to the kitchen and out the back. But the door to the hallway was closed. There was no way she or Zach could get it open and flee through it before Jack put bullets in their backs.

Silence reigned for what felt like an eternity. Then the man on the bullhorn said, "I'm coming in to talk to you, Jack. I'm unarmed."

"I know how this works, Russ," Jack said. "I know you can't cut a deal."

"What options do you have? The place is surrounded."

"Maybe I'll just clean house then."

Katrina took Zach's hand and squeezed it; he squeezed back. Her eyes fell on the shadowed form of Bandit, lying motionless, and she looked away.

"I just want to talk, Jack. Where's the harm in that?"

Jack seemed to consider this for a moment. Then he went to the door and inched it open a crack. "Come on in, Russ. But I'm not going to promise I'm not going to shoot you."

Jack turned to Katrina and Zach and waved the gun. "Get over to that wall, both of you."

"Jack—"

"Now!" he shouted.

They went to the far wall and hunkered down. Jack crouched behind them. Katrina thought his motivation was to get them all out of any possible line of fire through the front window. The seconds ticked by. The only sound she could hear was their breathing, Jack's the worst, and the rain on the roof. Finally, the door pushed farther open. A wedge of light, nothing more than a shade of gray fainter than that in the room, spilled across the hardwood floor. The outline of a man appeared, silhouetted against the storming night.

"Close the door behind you, Russ," Jack said.

The man obeyed. There was a sharp sound as the metallic tongue clicked home in the strike plate. Despite the shadows, Katrina could see the man named Russ was a little shorter than Jack, thick in the chest and shoulders, with hard features and a bald head.

He was dressed in navy slacks and a crisp white shirt, no blazer, revealing an empty gun holster.

Jack aimed the pistol at him. "How many outside?"

"Twelve."

"Don't bullshit me, Russ. This town's got a three-man police department. One's lying over there on the floor. That leaves two outside, the chief and some part-time senior citizen. You expect me to believe you brought a ten-man team with you?"

"The Agency's been itching to get you."

Katrina couldn't stand the not-knowing any longer. "Are you CIA?" she asked the man.

"Special Agent Russell Nowicki," he said. "I used to work with Jack Stone."

"Jack Stone?" She looked at Jack. "You said your name was Reeves."

Jack smiled humorlessly. "Guess I haven't been completely honest with you."

"And you worked for the CIA?"

"Jack was one of our top agents," Nowicki said. "He's served everywhere from Egypt to Iraq. A couple of years ago he was charged with destroying several tapes revealing the waterboarding of terror suspects. The Justice Department put together a case for his prosecution. A federal judge sentenced him to time behind bars. But Jack escaped custody while being escorted from the courthouse and has been underground ever since."

"I was serving my country, doing what was best for the Agency," Jack snarled, and there was a ferocity in his voice Katrina had not heard before. "If those tapes surfaced, the identity of the people involved would have been compromised. Lives would have been put in danger. And what thanks do I get?"

"You went against standing orders from the White House."

"Don't make it fucking political, Russ."

"Jesus, Jack. It's all political. Your cowboy shenanigans caused a real shitstorm. The bloody director was summoned before a grand jury after that *Post* story about the existence of secret CIA prisons overseas, which got the president in hot water. So tell me, Jack, how is it not political? Someone had to take the fall."

"They should have given me a medal," he said.

"Killing two cops wasn't the answer, Jack."

"What?" Katrina blurted. She was still trying to come to terms with what she was hearing. It was too much, too bizarre. "What do you mean, two cops?"

"That's how he escaped custody," Nowicki told her. "Took out the cops escorting him from the courthouse. Snapped one of their necks, then strangled the other with the handcuffs on his wrists. Took their car, drove off. Went completely off our radar—until this afternoon."

Katrina had gone numb all over. She had cared for Jack. She had slept with him.

A serial murderer. Maybe even a genuine sociopath.

Jack stood, yanking Katrina to her feet as well, holding her against him. "I want you to go back out there, Russ," he said, "and clear the street except for one car. Leave the keys in the ignition and the engine running. She's coming with me. I see anyone out there, I shoot her. I see anyone following us, I shoot her. Get it?"

"All right, Jack, if that's what you want. No problem. I'll clear the street. Just don't do anything stupid."

A squeak sounded from behind them.

Before Katrina knew what was happening, Jack squeezed off two rounds, dropping Nowicki to the floor. Then he was swiveling, releasing a firestorm of bullets through the hallway door. The door swung open and two men dressed in black combat gear tumbled head over heels into the living room.

Then Jack and Katrina were stumbling backward. Jack was still holding her, and she went down with him, landing on top of him. He dropped the pistol. She sprang off him and picked it up. She whirled around, holding it before her in both hands, backing up.

To her amazement, Zach had Jack in some kind of full nelson, and she realized Zach must have been the one who'd tugged Jack backward off his feet.

"Don't move, Jack!" she yelled.

He stared at her, his eyes burning with rage. "What are you going to do, Kat? Shoot me?"

"Yes," she said.

"Your hands are shaking so badly you couldn't hit the blind side of a barn."

"I swear I'll do it."

"No, I don't think you will." He broke Zach's hold on him and shoved him away. "You know why I don't think you will?"

"Shoot him!" Zach said, coming to stand beside her.

Jack's gaze flicked to him. "I'm starting to really regret not ending you in that shitty little basement of yours when I had the chance."

"Zach," Katrina said, never taking her eyes off Jack, "go outside and get some help."

"Who?"

"Anybody!"

"I'm not leaving you alone in here with him."

"Will wonders never cease," Jack said, taking a step toward one of the commandos lying on the floor—toward his weapon. "The Peeping Tom has a backbone."

"I said don't move, Jack!"

"You won't shoot me, Kat. You don't have murder in you. I've seen that firsthand." He crouched and picked up one of the two assault rifles on the floor. "Isn't that right?"

Fast as a snake, Jack swung the barrel toward her. She squeezed off three shots. The first missed, but the second plowed into Jack's chest and the third nicked his shoulder, spinning him about. He stumbled sideways, groping the wall for balance, then sliding down it, leaving a red streak on the beige paint. He coughed, spitting blood.

"Guess I was wrong," he mumbled, more blood bubbling from his mouth. "You're more like me than I thought."

He made a final guttural sound, then went still.

"Is he dead?" Zach asked, breaking her trance.

Time sped up. Sounds returned.

Katrina looped her arms around Zach's neck and held on to him tightly just as the front door banged open and more men in combat gear spilled into the room, aiming their guns and shouting orders.

EPILOGUE

Four months later.

Katrina was walking with Zach through the snow- and slush-covered sidewalk along Front Street. Leavenworth was more beautiful than ever when painted white and done up in Christmas lights and decorations. They passed King Ludwig's, the restaurant Jack had taken Katrina to on their first date, and she thought back to the night in her bungalow she'd been forced to shoot him. The police chief had arranged for Bandit to be taken to the town's vet, then he'd escorted them to the police station, which had gradually filled with FBI and CIA agents, all of whom drilled her with question after question about Jack and everything that led to the deadly climax at her place.

When she met with an attorney, she entered a guilty plea to a single-count indictment charging her with being an accessory to murder. She hadn't wanted to go through with a trial. She knew what she did, knew it was wrong, and took responsibility for it. At the sentencing, however, the deputy district attorney prosecuting the case recommended to the judge the minimum sentence in light of the circumstances of Jack Reeves's—or Jack Stone's—character, and her lack of a criminal record. The judge agreed, placing her on probation for one year.

And life in Leavenworth went on as usual. She returned to work at Cascade High School. She was not treated like a criminal as she'd thought she would be. In fact, most of her colleagues were sympathetic to what she'd been through. She spent most of her weekends fulfilling her penance, dividing her time among several charities, which required her to travel to several towns throughout Chelan County.

Father O'Donovan had only assigned her a hundred hours of community service, but she was enjoying what she was doing, she knew she was helping others, and she planned to make it a regular part of her life.

"So where's this place we're meeting Chris?" Katrina asked Zach. Crystal had called the day before to tell her she would be coming to Leavenworth for the weekend to see Zach, and they should all get together for dinner.

"Right there," Zach said, pointing to a small pub she hadn't yet visited.

He gestured for her to enter first, which she did—to a completely dark room. Before she could say anything, the lights flicked on and a chorus erupted in: "Surprise!"

Katrina's coworkers were huddled together in the center of the room, drinks raised in celebration. Crystal stepped from the crowd, kissed Zach on the cheek, then hugged Katrina. "Happy birthday!" she said.

After Katrina did the rounds, saying hi to everyone, she returned to Zach and Crystal and said, "Wow, Chris. I can't believe you organized this."

"I didn't," she said. "Zach did."

"Well, thanks, Zach," she said.

"I'm going to the bar," Crystal said. "What do you want, Kat?"

"Surprise me."

Crystal left, and Katrina said to Zach, "Chris tells me you've quit drinking?"

He shrugged. "New Year's resolution."

"What about your panic attacks?"

"My doctor gave me some meds to try. I'm taking things day by day. What about you?"

"My Ambien's working great."

"You know what I mean. New Year's resolution."

Katrina thought about it for a moment. "To run a background check on all potential boyfriends."

"Good one," Zach said. "By the way," he added, "have you made up your mind yet on whether you're going to stick around Leavenworth or head back to Seattle?"

"To be honest, I don't know. I guess I'm taking things day by day too."

"The students will miss you here."

"Seattle's big. I can be a wallflower."

"Nobody talks about Jack and all that stuff."

"They've been great. But—well, they still know."

He nodded, understanding. "I guess if you go to Seattle, you'll be closer to Chris too."

"She likes you, Zach," she said.

"I like her," he said.

"Take care of her."

"Of course," he said.

Crystal returned from the bar, carrying two cocktails and a can of ginger ale.

"What's this?" Katrina asked, taking one of the cocktails.

"No idea," Crystal said. "I asked the bar guy to surprise me." She raised her glass. "Happy birthday again, Kat," she said. "Thirty—yeesh!"

"Happy New Year's," she said in reply.

"To new starts," Zach said.

"To new starts," Crystal said.

Katrina repeated the toast as well, hoping it proved to be true.

ABOUT THE AUTHOR

Jeremy Bates

 USA TODAY and #1 AMAZON bestselling author Jeremy Bates has published more than twenty novels and novellas. They have sold more than one million copies, been translated into several languages, and been optioned for film and TV by major studios. Midwest Book Review compares his work to "Stephen King, Joe Lansdale, and other masters of the art." He has won both an Australian Shadows Award and a Canadian Arthur Ellis Award. He was also a finalist in the Goodreads Choice Awards, the only major book awards decided by readers.

Made in the USA
Las Vegas, NV
19 October 2023

79316078R00173